Praise for
'Too Much of the Wrong Thing'

At first glance Claire Hopple's stories appear delightfully off kilter, even laugh-out-loud funny, but the flashes of wisdom start early in this collection and they don't stop. This is a world of constant disorientation where people aim for connection and gamble on intimacy, no matter how precarious. Hopple's small towns are in decline and her families are fragile. Everybody lives here: older relatives who unravel or disappear; a sibling tipping over into frightening criminality; three generations of women with the same name in the same house who manage to lose each other; a hitchhiker who proves the lie of American life; a couple of friends from childhood, forever connected in a web of communal memory. After watching Hopple's characters question the scripts they've been handed, we are left to marvel at the hard work of being lost.

~ Jan Stinchcomb, author of *Find the Girl*

Claire Hopple's short story collection is a nuanced tug o'war of sardonic words and the playful triteness of the world wherein everything is the same, introspection spawns introspection, and life itself is a non sequitur. *Too Much of the Wrong Thing* is a beautifully woven collection of pale scenes and strange adult feelings that demands to be read.

~ Mallory Smart, author of *I Want To Feel Happy But I Only Feel__*

Claire Hopple is a fantastic writer. A killer, really. Her characters take bubble baths when their moms die; keep porcupines as pets; chew nicotine gum but still smoke because they want to capitalize on addiction. Her stories are gold plated in form, but punk at the core. *Too Much of the Wrong Thing* is a going away party for yourself.

~ Bud Smith, author of *Dust Bunny City*

Claire Hopple's *Too Much of the Wrong Thing* is a wonderful collection. She explores perspective and emotion with dexterity. Her stories remain in the reader's consciousness accumulating into a tapestry of vibrant characters and prose that isn't afraid to pack a punch.

~ Dylan Taylor, author of *101 Adages for the Millennial*

TOO MUCH

of the

WRONG THING

Claire Hopple

TRUTH SERUM PRESS

TRUTH SERUM PRESS

First published as a collection November 2017

Truth Serum Press
4 Warburton Street
Magill SA 5072
Australia

Email: truthserumpress@live.com.au
Website: http://truthserumpress.net
Truth Serum Press catalogue: http://truthserumpress.net/catalogue/

Cover design by Matt Potter

ISBN: 978-1-925536-33-1

Also available as an eBook
ISBN: 978-1-925536-34-8

for Unk

Contents

Bars of Soap

Your mother died and you didn't cry. You were always afraid of this. You tried, felt like you should, but couldn't. The only way you knew you were upset was when your boyfriend said she always had a weird smell, you slapped him on the cheek. This made you less nervous, except for the fact that you really do slap like a girl, just as your brother had always taunted.

The same day she died, you went home to take a bath. You thought sulking and soaking were similar enough words. You added bubbles because you thought that was appropriate, respectful in a way. People only take bubble baths when they're truly sad. Plus, you didn't have to stare down at your naked body in a seated position. You eased your insecurities by thinking this wasn't a very flattering posture for anyone. You stared at the bubbles instead, which seemed quite whimsical and flighty instead of respectful like you'd hoped.

You remembered that you gain a certain confidence in the bathtub that you can't carry with you anywhere else. You created an excellent rebuttal to one of your mother's back-pocket phrases. She liked to say the opposite of trite phrases, like, "Things really are as they seem," and "Count all of your chickens before they hatch. How else would you prepare?" In the bathtub, you shouted, desperately wanted to tell her, "Things aren't always as they seem. Look at the word 'lugubrious'. It sounds like what happens to your mouth after you eat saltwater taffy." But she was not the bubble on the surface. She was probably at home drinking wine and wearing your father's sweatpants. You shook your head, correcting yourself. No. She is not. Anymore.

*

A few days before, you stopped at a coffee shop near work. Unlike your coworkers, this wasn't part of your routine. Three people stood in line ahead of you. A man was first in line. You heard him mutter his order, a chai latte with soy milk. Maybe you should just get that. At least that sounded like what you should get.

He moved out of line. A mom with a child singing quite loudly was next. Wait, that's only two in front now, you thought. You frantically stared at the chalkboard above but nothing morphed into something recognizable.

The child continued, half-singing, half-screaming. "Up where they walk, up where they run," her voice cracked and lilted but flowed back up to pitch, "up where they stay all day in the sunnnn!"

Her mother shushed her and simply pointed to

someone else's very large to-go cup of coffee, as if words were just too much, as if mothers were now excused from speaking, some taciturn societal guideline specially made for those with little girls who liked to squeal out parts from *The Little Mermaid* in public places.

A girl with a bouncy ponytail was next. A girl with a bouncy ponytail was the only thing between you and the frowning barista. Between you and what now seemed to be a rather serious and existential decision. Should you get tea? Your mother keeps little packets of Darjeeling and Earl Grey stuffed in the sugar canister with her Camel Lights. The canister always sits on the counter next to empty bottles of white zinfandel.

At four o'clock every afternoon, she always says, "I need a little zin, it's my zen," and retires to the living room with glass of wine in hand, just in time for Oprah. She laughs at Oprah. A lot. Especially when Oprah is in the middle of saying something dramatic, like, "How did it feel to leave your husband for a woman?" This has always concerned you.

"Miss? Excuse me?"

You were at the counter. You decided to just see what kind of order came out of your mouth. Like a free association game. Like lying on a sofa in a psychoanalyst's office. Like giving an oral report in third grade about the *Goosebumps* book you stole from your brother's room the night before.

The barista blinked, then stared. He was about to turn to a coworker to ask what to do with you, so you opened your mouth.

"Wish I could be, part of that woorrrrld," you belted out.

You covered your mouth. Bells jingled on the door handle as you ran out.

*

You decided that baths should be part of your regular routine. It reminded you of your personal life: you seemed to enjoy sitting in your own filth and over-thinking. You thought about your boyfriend this time. He is a professor at a community college down the street.

He is not pipe tobacco, paisley neckties, dusty books. He is tacos at midnight, video games between classes, sarcastic and inappropriate t-shirts at your annual family reunion. You washed him off in the tub, too. You thought of him, holding the snifter glass up to his tiny nose, imparting to you the intricacies of brandy. You shuddered in the scalding water.

You remembered your theory as a child, that people with the best character always have the most impossibly shaped noses. The larger and more misshapen, the better. At that moment, you thought you were exactly right as a child; that you've always been exactly right about everything.

*

You were seven. You were about to have a friend over for the first time. This made you very excited. Your mother vacuumed the weary carpet right before she was supposed to arrive. You could see the lines, the obvious attempt. You knew even at that age the desperation that seeped up from the plowed fields of carpet. You whined to your mother until she broke, until she grabbed her ashtray and dumped her ashes all over the carpet.

*

She dumped her ashes all over the carpet.

*

You were still in the habit of baths a few months later, but you added a rum and coke to the routine. Or two or three. You didn't know why you kept buying bars of soap instead of body wash. Bars of soap disappear too quickly. You thought it was a bit dangerous to be drinking in a tub. Maybe you needed a life vest. It swallowed you as a kid, jabbing your chin as you bobbed in the lake water, covering up the edges of your thin-lipped mouth, smothering your hot little breaths.

So much for preserving life.

*

The day your mother died, you went to your professor boyfriend's basketball game. You weren't sure how men over 30 started one of these leagues. You always thought these kind of things were for kids still in school. You sat on the stiff bleacher and made up a backstory for each of the players. That one is in a Phish cover band and donates plasma too frequently.

It was winter and you were queasy from the cold weather. The heat in the gym was overwhelming and you weren't sure which was worse – inside or outside. Your sweater was itchy. The vintage heater seemed to collapse your lungs and suck up all the remains of moisture from your elbows and knuckles. When you moved your arms, your elbow skin caught on the wool of your sweater. You had no idea what number jersey your boyfriend was.

After the game, you gave him a hug and congratulated him, but you were really congratulating him on how sweaty he was, since you weren't paying attention to the game. He didn't seem to notice. You wondered if they still went out for ice cream after games like you used to do after your brother's. You asked your boyfriend this in a weird pitch, attempting to break out of condescension.

A fellow teammate behind him said it had switched

from ice cream to beer. He turned around and they looked at each other conspiratorially.

*

She dumped her ashes all over the carpet.

Quilled

The horde of porcupines began to form not long after Labor Day, when we were so freed up from our labors we forgot to feed them. Our children had insisted on baby porcupines as pets; everyone was getting them. And once one of us on the street got one, you know the rest of us wouldn't hear the end of it until we did, too.

Our children with hair like silks hidden inside corn stalks were suddenly holding these breathing balls of spikes. These sheltered sons and daughters of ours asked for and received living weapons, even if they were in miniature.

Their quills lay flat unless they're threatened, our children explained. They're just little babies, they cooed. But some of us were quilled in interesting places nonetheless, our own form of acupuncture. And we kept stepping on the shed quills in our bare feet in the night, just trying to use the bathroom. And mostly, we were getting tired of them because, scientifically (we stopped letting our kids do the research and did some ourselves), they're rodents. The third largest rodents in the world.

These baby porcupines grew up and they were no longer baby porcupines but just regular porcupines, and it all seemed very strange. So we set them free to wander the sidewalks, climb our fenced-in trees, no less prickly than the rest of us, really.

We released them and we could hear children wailing from houses with cracked open windows like half-hearted sirens.

*

Since the upheaval, they have moved to the trees in our backyards that lead to the woods, hanging from limbs, nibbling on bark. At night, they venture out to Mrs. Grunewald's lawn and eat the tips of her begonias, though no one has actually witnessed it. They make labyrinthine patches in the shrubs, but some of us think they look better that way.

*

We saw Ava and Tomorrow Jones talk over the fence sometimes. They lived right next door to each other. Mrs. Grunewald liked to overhear things but she didn't have anything conclusive regarding an affair. They liked to talk about music, she said. She delivered an example conversation to some of us.

"You'd be surprised what can be used as instruments. How everyday items can be so *percussive*. So musical," Tomorrow Jones supposedly said.

"It all sounds very resourceful," Ava supposedly said back, leaning into the shared fence a bit more.

Ava's husband, Roland, ignored Tomorrow Jones. But not completely. It was more like Roland would pretend to ignore him, we gathered. Like he might be jealous of him. Like he might think his wife was having an affair with him. We wondered too, of course, but like Roland, we did not actually want to find out. We didn't want to be implicated in the alleged entanglement; we wanted simply to wonder about it.

We knew that Ava was writing her dissertation on American Society's Response to Single Adult Females (or some outrageous title like that) when she met Roland. She couldn't finish it because her field work had been compromised. They always raved about their honeymoon out west. We could imagine their initial passion: the patter of their rinsed out bathing suits hanging over the resort shower curtain rod like a distant rain. Or like a clock's sonorous insistence of time.

But Roland's new job made him travel frequently and Ava doesn't like being alone. She would always talk about her runs through the neighborhood, how she always runs by the house with the high fence no one has seen behind. Every time, she hears what must be the clacking of dog claws against what must be a deck, following at the same pace as her, just being able to hear the breath and claws, not seeing, but feeling the dog's attempted greeting.

Roland would call when she lay panting and stretching in the yard after her runs and the connection would be bad. She would end up talking very loudly to make up for it when he was driving through cavernous tunnels on a distant expressway.

"I can't get through to you," we would hear her say, still out of breath.

*

Tomorrow Jones had a limp. He acquired a cane with a sterling silver panther on top. The panther was frozen mid-leap, agile, much like Tomorrow used to be. He was older but still attractive. One of those guys who looked especially good with gray hair. We knew he was an artist or poet of some kind. We heard from Mrs. Grunewald that he was also a new adjunct professor at the university and only had one or two advanced workshops to cover. But there was also a rumor that he was retired and mowed lawns in graveyards to pass the time. We knew for sure that he received many packages in oblong shapes, which were left on his porch beside his front door for hours at a time. Tomorrow had a painted tin roof that dinged loudly when it rained.

*

The porcupines liked to moan and grunt in the trees behind the neighborhood. It would wake up some of us lighter sleepers. More disconcerting were the coughing sounds they would occasionally make. We thought there were extra phlegmy intruders in our homes at first. Our street was close to the hospital so we were already used to the whine of sirens. It didn't take us that long to adjust.

*

Most of us stayed in during the winter. Someone would be telling one of us a serious, dramatic story when we really just wanted to go in from the cold, or put down our heavy grocery bags, or scratch our knee, but we would feel that was inappropriate during such a heavy story and as we weighed whether or not it was appropriate, our need ever increasing, we would have accidentally stopped listening to the important story. Which was way worse than knee scratching.

Then again, a few of us had stopped trying to converse with each other a long time ago. Instead, we would watch each other. Or we'd watch the old man who hunted through the garbage cans in the alley. Roland got into it with him one day and we couldn't believe it. He'd just returned from a business trip and he confronted the guy about passing over his cans. He said the old man would spend a lot more time sifting through others' garbage and would barely lift the lid on Roland's or pass over it completely. Roland asked the guy if there was something wrong with his garbage. Supposedly, the man shrugged and said it was all filled with candy bar wrappers and he wasn't interested in empty candy bar wrappers.

Ava had a flexible job so we wondered why she didn't go with Roland on his trips. She didn't want to leave, well, because, she didn't want to leave. That was as articulate as she could be, at least to us.

*

We continued to hear whines and groans through the winter, which was replaced with a lot of shuffling in the summer. Then Mrs. Grunewald's grandson, an aspiring zoologist, told us that during mating season, the male porcupine dances for the female, then sprays his urine over her head, aswirl with desire.

*

At the end of the summer, during rush hour, cars were stopped on the street. Our cars' engines hummed in harmony, idling, one in front of the other. There were two fire trucks and a police car blocking the way. Our eyes grew sore from staring. We all hoped, individually in our own cars, that it wasn't *our* house on fire.

It turned out to be the home of Tomorrow Jones. The fire was being investigated. The term "suspected arson" hung from our tongues like a fatty morsel. One of us knew the fire chief. The fire chief's wife cut people's hair in her basement, gave some people perms.

The eastern portion of his house was charred. It wasn't all that bad. They got to the flames relatively quickly. But we saw the moving trucks shortly after. Ava gave him an intricately wrapped present before he moved, some sort of going away gift. We weren't sure if it was out of pure kindness or love or if she was thanking him for leaving.

The house is being restored. We now hear hammers and humming equipment and loud, mechanized slams when we're not hearing the porcupines. A double-jointed woman who wears a lot of Lululemon appears to be moving in. None of us have introduced ourselves yet.

15 Signs of the Cocktail Generation

1. She thought about calling her parents but remembered that it was too late there. Time zones seemed so unnatural to her and yet they made sense. She had always been an hour behind them anyway.

2. She often stared in wonder at her neighbor: always in pajama pants, walking a sad piece of cotton that was supposedly a dog, stomach distended while everything else on his body was depleted to the bone, flat affect and impotent eyes. But her neighbor would disappear behind a tree line and she would return to whatever she was doing. Then the leaves fell and she could see him all too well.

3. She received a Christmas card in the mail from a high school friend, but when she opened the envelope there was nothing inside. She must have forgotten to put the card in, she told herself, still swaddled in her winter coat though she had been inside the house for about an hour. Throwing away the empty envelope, she recalled how this friend used to come over and they would lie on the couch at opposite ends, TV screen flickering in

their irises, feet touching. Feet exchanging temperature back and forth, hot and cold, cold and hot, but rarely comfortable or the same.

4. Her mother was the only person left on earth who still clipped articles from a real newspaper and reminded her to buy Forever stamps right before the price rose again.

5. After she had graduated from college, her father had asked her what was next. There was a substantial sum of family money for her to use for anything, but it seemed more like something looming in a closet than a gift. She replied that she wanted to open a boutique downtown and sell things as pretty as what hung in her own closet. But he told her, no, boutiques never made any profit. People are too comfortable in the enchanting atmosphere. They are satisfied to look and dreamily float back onto the street. If you want to do retail, he told her, you must open up a chain store in a mall. The thumping heartbeat of music, piercing lights and enclosed walls make people Darwinian. They must gather up as many items as possible for survival. It truly feels like the end.

6. The boyfriend kept all the cards she gave him, though in a box in the basement. His collegiate intramural soccer trophies were on a shelf in his living room.

7. Little red pimples formed along her jawline from constantly leaning on her hands, as if she needed the extra support as she read the weighty matters on her screen all day. She felt too old for pimples.

8. Growing up, her father, mostly an investor and steward of the family money pile, chose to spend his time developing elaborate meals for the family. He would make these pasta dishes effortlessly. San Marzano tomatoes like delicious, fleshy hearts with cavatappi noodles. The noodles were so ornate and whimsical looking, and surprisingly hollow in the middle. They were his favorite noodle. Sometimes she would sneak into the pantry before dinner and suck on the raw noodles, then crunch down when it was softened a bit and safe for the teeth, hoping it would calm her appetite. Her father would spend hours preparing and she would swallow the plate in seven minutes or less.

9. At his desk, her father used to sign checks – Graham L. Gershon – in a flourish, proudly displaying what seemed like unnecessary consonants. She used to sit beside him and scrawl her signature in crayon with the harried desperation for enthusiasm found at a New Year's Eve party.

10. The dentist gave her a night guard to put on before falling asleep to keep her from gnawing away at herself.

11. Most days, she got up early before work to sit by the window and read. Occasionally, birds or squirrels would venture near her window. They would show off on a high branch or make these swift movements unnatural for a human to make, seemingly just for her, and she would assume she was Snow White.

12. Returning to her parent's home, she always regarded the Mantel of Picture Frames. On the right side, her sister smiling on her wedding day alongside her groom. No one could remember the family before he was around and nobody wanted to. Then another frame with the same two people, this time three kids: one on each lap and one on the floor, tantrum filling up in his eyes. The left side of the mantel was her: the high school graduation picture. Beside it, a picture of her three nephews.

13. Her sister would call to remind her to send a birthday present to a certain cousin, or to call Grandma, who just had surgery. She never remembered these things on her own but was still able to feel connected to her grandmother with dementia. She often couldn't remember who she was or where she was or what she was doing or to whom she belonged, either.

14. She could never meet her friend at the movies because the friend was incapable of showing up until halfway through or would wander into a different movie that looked more interesting. She learned to go to the movies by herself so that spending time with friends might involve actually seeing and speaking with them.

15. Strangers at parties often asked her about her rather traditional job, surprised, knowing about the inheritance. She chose to reply tritely, "It keeps me out of trouble," then gulp her cocktail. She would not say the truth; that having free time would prove she wasn't

capable of getting into trouble, which is far more sinful. The overwhelming amount of sugar in the cocktail often made the alcohol affect her differently, skipping the dreamy stage altogether and making her disoriented and sloppy.

Craigslist Missed Connection

Career Woman in Red Dress in
Downtown Hampton Inn Bar
gender: male
body: average
status: single

I met you the day that my eyes changed color. I have to think that means something. Like when I saw a bear cross the highway, its rounded muscles rippling under its fur, and that same week I got a call that yes, I did get that teaching position.

It was rather unexpected; your whole life having brown eyes and you wake up in your early 30s and they're changed to an icy blue. I thought I was hallucinating. Then I poked my eyes to check if someone had snuck colored contacts underneath my lids while I was asleep. No such luck.

I had nothing against blue eyes. It's just that they weren't *my* eyes anymore. I noticed yours were a piercingly beautiful blue, so obviously I have no problems with that.

This must be a sign of eye cancer, I convinced myself. So I called and made an appointment with my eye doctor, who also happens to be one of my closest friends. This fact was depressingly convenient, like getting hit by an ambulance.

The receptionist asked me the typical questions. I wanted to make panicky shrieks into her ear but instead I kept getting quieter with each word. I was so quiet by the end of the conversation that she kept asking me to repeat myself.

This eye doctor friend of mine, his name is Troy Carlisle. You'll probably meet him soon. I was wary of Troy at first because when I met him, he spoke in an Australian accent, and I learned during our second meeting that the accent was not real. Troy Carlisle grew up in Billings, Montana. I'm still not sure why he would feel the need to lie about that. He also told me during our second meeting that he views all work as some form of prostitution. I have a hard time disagreeing but I didn't necessarily want him anywhere near my eyes. It turns out he's very skilled, has a great reputation in the community and even cuts me a special deal.

While waiting for Troy, I feigned aloofness in front of the walls, the clinical cabinets. I saw images in the wood grain of the closed door like a Rorschach because there was nothing else to look at lying in that chair, waiting. The chair that had me tipped back just enough to where I couldn't get up easily. Right where they wanted me. I saw an angry frog in the door, a stony-eyed lion. A small balloon in the top corner close to the hinge. You can analyze that if you want to.

When Troy finally strolled in, I did not ask him all of the burning questions I had. I let the paranoia bubble up and release into the air. He eventually revealed to me that I have pigmentary glaucoma. So not cancer. And I had even practiced my rueful look, as if I were reflecting on all the poor lifestyle choices I had made that led me to eye cancer.

"It's not that bigga deal, Holt," he told me. My eye doctor talks to me this way.

*

I used this pigmentary glaucoma as an excuse to call off work for the rest of the week. I was still unsettled, but a bit relieved. I did not want to face my classroom. The students as harsh and unforgiving as the overhead lights.

They're still better than when I was temping at an academy for homeschoolers. The contradiction in that name is not lost on me. Those feral homeschoolers with their rapidly beating hearts and injurious gazes. I half expected them to be huddled in the corner when I walked in, hunched over torn off hunks of bread. You have no idea.

I shouldn't have been as shocked as I was with my new pair of blue eyes. Things pretty much go the opposite way I intend constantly, and I've grown comfortable with acting as if that's exactly what was planned. Things continue whether you like them or not and what exactly are you supposed to do with that?

What I did with it was, well, I went to a bar. Original, I know. But I went to a bar at a hotel (as you well know), so I had my own spin on alcoholism. I thought hotel bars were more exotic. They gave me the feeling of traveling, of doing something transcendent, without having to do very much at all.

And I can't say it wasn't a great plan, because there you were, at the bar. I wouldn't leave you to have your drink in peace like you probably wanted. You were in town for a conference, I recall, but the details are blurry. Everything was blurry.

But I do remember that you were a professional of some kind. You had a job and it was the kind of job that you did when you wanted to do something on purpose. Was it a nutrition conference you were attending? Are you a nutritionist? I ask because I remember you talking about fermented food and how good it was for people. How the nutrients intensify as the food starts to decompose. And I said, "I think I can relate." And you laughed and said you didn't know what that meant. It was like something softened in my stomach and strengthened in my chest at the same time. A tearing down of a blockade and a building up of something whole. I tricked us both with my contentment, for a moment.

I asked you to accompany me to dinner. You paused before answering, longer than I would have liked. I'm not sure how we ended up talking about our family histories and how exactly it came up that we might share the same father. I'm just not convinced. There are probably hundreds of Jeremy Crawfords who fought in Vietnam and then settled in New York afterwards.

At least we should do research, study genealogies, before we arrive at any conclusions.

I excused myself to go to the bathroom. My new glaucoma medication gave me an upset stomach and it was the first time I experienced it. Maybe you think I fled due to the strange turn in our conversation. I assure you I was actually using the toilet. When I came back, it was to an empty table.

Couldn't you at least have left your phone number?

Your room number?

Your hometown?

I'm typing this on my deck while I watch my neighbors put up Halloween decorations. "Move the skeleton to the left," the husband says, motioning to the wife as she teeters out the second story window with her hands grasped firmly against its ribcage. The husband has a nice sweater on. I can tell he keeps his sweaters in a drawer rather than a closet because the sweater has a firm crease down the middle with little feathered wisps of creases along the sides from it not being perfectly folded.

It seems rather infelicitous to me, all of this death as decor. Proudly displaying all of these things that are normally considered grotesque. I know I've seen plenty of Halloween decorations over the years but I guess I haven't really seen them like I am seeing them now. But the more I'm looking at it, the more it starts to seem completely appropriate.

Projector

The boy sat in the hallway, staring. His snot created a tributary into his open mouth. He kicked at the air. Ranger watched him fidget until the principal walked out of the front office.

"Mr. Keys?" she smiled.

"Yes," he said, shaking her hand.

"I'm Mrs. Plimpton, the head principal. It's a pleasure to meet you," she said.

She smoothed her hands over her blazer primly and then began her tour of the school.

This school: his last school. It was just as well. He couldn't handle taking the bus again. Those hand pulls like a line of nooses waiting for necks. Plus, technology had changed things too much. The satisfying click of the next slide had been replaced with the impotent click of the mouse over the play button on the computer file. He longed for his Carousel 5400, each 35 mm slide placed upside down and backwards in order to display correctly on screen. The sole glow of the projector's eye to him the purest form of sight. It now lived in a box in his basement next to his Stairmaster.

Before his presentations, Ranger always turned off the lights himself as a way of mentally preparing. He never remembered turning the switches off and on anymore, in gymnasiums, auditoriums, even in his own home. This secretly terrified him. He assumed it was because he turned switches so often that it was no longer memorable, some sort of brain shortcut. But in his 67 years, he has done many activities repeatedly, which means that soon his whole life would be as unrecallable as the flicking of a switch. This had ultimately led him to his decision to retire.

*

The assembly before the last one was at a nearby middle school. The music teacher made an announcement before his presentation about a fundraiser for Kenyan refugees, but the middle school brains were cumulonimbus romances, stratus wisps of narcissism, and no one even listened to the teacher. Middle schools were his least favorite.

Faye had moved out the day before the middle school assembly, which was fine. She would talk incessantly of children, but not of having her own. Some people treated dogs like children, but Faye treated children like, well, not exactly dogs but some kind of pet: she would find them adorable at distances and want them around in certain ideal settings as accessories, and then she would pat them on their heads in farewell.

Right before she left, she told him, "I don't want to cry because I would be crying about the wrong things." He wanted to see her again, not because he thought they should still be together, but so that he could find out what those things were.

Ranger had never married and Faye was his longest relationship. Growing up with a twin had forced him into unreasonable standards for companionship. They had participated in a twin study as children to make some extra cash but the results had been inconclusive. Not all the dependent variables had been addressed. Or was it the independent variables? He could never remember.

Ranger's twin Roger had won the lottery a few years ago, and the following week had been seriously injured in an accident on the interstate, ultimately becoming a quadriplegic. Ranger thought this was somehow worse than if his brother had died. At least if he had passed away Ranger could still relate to him. The lottery winnings covered all the medical expenses and provided a sizeable, handicap-accessible mansion for Roger and his wife.

*

"So your website said you have several different types of presentations," said Mrs. Plimpton.

"Yes, depending on the age range and audience size, I can cover National Parks, various environmental causes and animal adaptations."

"Adaptations?"

"Basically how fish, birds, bugs, and other species adapt to their respective environments: gathering food, self-defense, even how they camouflage themselves."

"Fascinating."

She showed him the joint gymnasium/auditorium last.

"There's been a surge of new jobs at the local plant and a lot of engineers and their young families are moving here, so our classrooms have become overcrowded," she explained, standing in front of the gym doors like a sentry. "This forced us into sectioning off the gym. I hope you understand. We should have a nice spot cleared before your show tomorrow."

She opened the doors and he peeked in on what looked like large cubicles. Children's voices echoed shrilly like he imagined the gym whistle used to.

He thanked her for the tour. On his way out, he overheard a tutor working with a young student, teaching that "someone" was one word and "no one" was two. A child whose constructs were probably still drawn with thick, simple lines. A child who could not possibly understand how the one word could be in a different category from the other. The tutor was growing frustrated and Ranger could feel electrical pulses of anger emanating from the open classroom door. Her frustration was some kind of feeling directed at the child, albeit negative, but that was a start.

*

The next morning, he waited at the bus stop in the rain. He knew there were different types of rain and that the types all tried to communicate different memories, ideas, places. This particular rain felt like Boston, though he was in Pittsburgh. It was chilly, brooding, almost ominous without striking fear, and with a sense of history. Substantial and ancient in its humidity. Like yellowed pages and sweaters kept in a chest in a forgotten room.

This Boston-type rain reminded him that he used to schedule assemblies nationally, used to actually see places like Boston. Now he just covered Western PA. No, he corrected himself, later this afternoon he would be retired. He could go anywhere. He could go somewhere.

*

Ranger was safe in the gymnasium's fetid, sticky embrace. Mrs. Plimpton had just introduced him to the new assistant principal. The assistant principal was even wearing a nametag. She was the only one wearing a nametag.

He started setting up, connecting wires, sipping from his water bottle, when he was handed a mug of instant coffee by CHERYL LAWRENCE, ASST. PRINCIPAL. Pal was underlined. He assumed Plimpton was behind this. All of this. The mug had a child's finger-painted handprint in the school's colors. The other side had the school's mascot, a dragon, with the slogan, "Educating tomorrow's leaders today" below its fire-breathing mouth.

CHERYL LAWRENCE had eyes with pupils and irises indistinguishable in color, so that Ranger didn't know exactly where she was looking. It gave her an inhuman, morbid appearance. Other than her eyes, she looked ordinary.

Kids shuffled in and found their seats. He switched off the lights and opened his slideshow file titled "preserving_habitats.mp4". His encyclopedic voice rolled on into the dark room and it was all muscle memory from there.

A few teachers came up to thank him after it was over. One remarked that it was a large improvement over the last assembly, which featured a nutritional opera starring a stalk of broccoli and a banana with a noteable falsetto.

He saw Faye in the back. She strolled up to the stage.

"I didn't want to miss your last show," she said.

That was one thing about her, her thoughtfulness. He would miss that. He could use more of that, learn from it. She showed him a picture of her family reunion, one of their last outings together. Her nephew was seated in a high chair at a table full of adults, Ranger and Faye included. The table was littered with bottles.

"Look at him playing with all the adults," she mused, and for a moment Ranger thought she was talking about him.

Cross-Pollination

The table rocked when you pressed against it. The chair swayed a bit, too. You weren't sure if it was the floor, the foundation, the furniture. You were beginning to feel used to the unsteady.

Then Lexi came down the stairs and told you that Griffin had started chewing nicotine gum simply to cross-pollinate her addictions. She told you this neutrally, admitted it might be working on her. She moved her hair away from her face like she was lifting and spreading a curtain.

"Ah, you should get rid of him. He is a snaggletoothed stranger at best," you thought you replied.

But your mind had not been fully brought back from the table and you had actually just shouted "Ridiculous!" long after she sauntered back up the stairs.

You had been letting the friendship drift for a while anyway. You had been somewhat piratical with her life stories at a few parties and felt guilty about it. You felt you had to make up for your suburban history; it seemed like more of a papery past.

And really, what is there to talk about at those parties

you go to? You're not sure why you still get invited. Things just fall out of your mouth and when you listen to others, all you can think about is whether you are clenching your mouth together so uneasily that it's hard for the other person to look at you.

Plus, at those gatherings you had to introduce yourself to people you already knew and figure out how much is appropriate to reveal that you already knew. A dizzying game.

What you needed was honesty but a controlled kind of honesty, you told yourself. But you only seemed to find the extremes.

You got up from the rocky table and found that your mother had called. Sometimes, when your mother beckoned you back home, you would run into someone at the grocery store with a child's face somewhere inside an adult face and you would try to remember.

High school was so far away now that you couldn't tell apart the married names from the maiden names of people whose Lite Brites and action figures will forever be floating around in the back of your head. And those who from the wretched convention of divorce flitted back and forth between the maiden and the not, you long ago committed to calling them by their first names. That is, if they ever appeared from out of their societal crevices. They would push out babies to perpetuate the code and then they would complain about how the new code was just like them.

You put your phone away, knowing you would call your mother back later. You worried about being late to work. You were late to work.

You thought about your stringent boss. An opportunity squelched. Something rushed through the veins in your arms, in a line down to your wrists. You thought the time you arrived at work was one of those things, like graduating from high school. If you succeed in pulling it off, you are a responsible member of society. But if you fail, then you are muttered about, put into a category. There is nothing in between.

How can there be nothing in between?

You managed to step out of the house and saw a few neighbors on their porches and in their yards, which made you remember that other people live so close to you, doing the same things you do.

Then you were explaining a project to a coworker at the office, gradually panicking, your brain piloting the words coming out of your mouth. You found yourself saying the word "wistfully" to sound casual and smart amid the panic, a word you had read and then heard someone say all in the same day. You were saying it simply from exposure. Words tend to pop up serially like that and your brain follows through with it, communicating lazily. Always shortcuts and short circuits with that brain of yours. A brain so unmotivated that it remembers commercial jingles rather than branches of government. No wonder you were panicking.

You must have appeased the person because you heard her admitting, "Yeah, I mean, I was expecting to have my own agency at this point. Ah, well."

"Big things always come along more slowly than you want them to," you coached, though you did not know exactly who you were coaching. Those big things seem so important and yet the mundane, smaller things always take over, so that you feel as if you are constantly recovering from the mundane. How do people even take care of themselves?

The shifty table was waiting for you expectantly when you returned home.

Lexi opened the door languidly, glancing at her sandaled feet rather than at you. She was moving out, she explained, rather, moving in with Griffin.

Now that it was happening it seemed so clear that it was always going to happen. Why didn't you anticipate this?

You stammered out a faint goodbye, tried to remember people mowing their lawns and watching their televisions a few feet away. You tried to remember this wasn't a boyfriend breaking up with you, just a roommate moving.

Lexi's items lingered for a few weeks, then dissipated. Piece by piece, you found things to replace the empty. You collected furniture, curated bits of life to hang on the wall. You built yourself an environment so desirable so that you would stay there, never want to be anywhere else. To be a proper recluse. But as things gathered and started to look almost beautiful, you just felt compelled to show someone.

Signs of Futility

1. Two small dogs next door yipping at a garbage truck from behind a fence.

Relentlessly blinking lights outside on an otherwise dark street. The uniformed officers sitting inside these flickering vehicles were just vaporous shadows at this point, but I couldn't help but watch for them to emerge.

I figured they were here because of my brief period of armed robbery. It had seemed too easy at the time so I expected something like this. Either that or they wanted to ask me about the note I found in my house. Regardless, my shirt clung to my back from the sweat. I am not one who knows how to play it cool. I don't think people who know how to play it cool would call it 'playing it cool' to begin with.

I was trying to decide which room I would direct them into and I was clueless. Each one seemed wrong. I couldn't decipher this basic thing. Maybe we could use the room nobody ever goes in. The living room is too devoted to comfort to be appropriate. Certainly my bedroom would not be a good choice. The entryway is too cold, too suspicious.

The note I found was just the culmination of a series of incidents, really. I would return from the market or from visiting my mother or from knocking off a distant convenience store (if it was during the aforementioned period), and I would find dirt stains in the bathtub. I didn't use the bathtub, and I mostly lived alone.

I say mostly because my daughter stays with me every once in a while. She is a teenager and all she seems to have time for is her face. She just stares at her face and its pores in the mirror. Cleansing, scrubbing, using these adhesive strips that pull and stretch, popping, pushing skin together, tearing at it so that it leaves little nail marks on her nose, dabbing, drying off with a towel until her entire face is blotchy and puffy, as if she had lost a fight. I'm afraid those genes came from my side of the family.

But she doesn't stay all that often. Then I found some blankets that smelled of some perfumed oil strewn about my couch and easy chair. Then there was the small patch in my backyard that looked like someone had started a fire.

I wasn't all that concerned because I just rent this place. When I moved in, I never changed the locks. I heard from Mrs. Dunnivan that the previous tenants were overly hospitable and all their friends came and went as they pleased. I figure these friends must be in some pitiable state so I don't really mind. It's kind of nice to think people are getting some use out of the place when I'm out; not letting it sit empty and quiet. I don't have nice things.

That is, I didn't really mind until I found the note on my nightstand. It was in a frantic scrawl so it was hard to read.

PLEASE HELP FIND MY DAUGHTER BIANCA

Since there were no punctuation marks I had to assume that Bianca was the daughter and not the author. The author had torn a page from my copy of *Breakfast of Champions* to make this note, which set me off a little. The person could have taken a page from my abandoned Sudoku book instead.

When the police officers knocked I wasn't able to get a word in. Turns out they were investigating a noise complaint and they had the wrong address. The dogs next door didn't even bark once at them.

*

2. Throwing something heavy into a hotel room trash can and expecting the weakly knotted liner to stay in place.

I threw away the invitation to the neighborhood block party, then took it back out. I had just changed the bag so it was fairly clean. I had stolen the can from an old motel I visited once in Florida. I become a kleptomaniac when I have too much tequila. I usually skip these neighborhood events but I remembered that Mrs. Dunnivan mentioned that some of my house squatters attended these parties, as if they legitimately lived on the street.

My house was the only rented one on this street, technically on the nicer side of town, so I didn't like to be reminded of that. But I wanted to help the person who left the note. A daughter is not a thing to lose.

I imagined this was the kind of party where local politicians were offered measly bribes and minor affairs played themselves out to a willing audience. I squeezed myself into my best and itchiest sweater and walked up the hill.

The party was at the home of Claudia and Lincoln Moon. They lived next to the deserted house. It would have been called haunted if it weren't a new build where no one had died. People trickled in and out of ownership, never staying. It was the only one on the street like this and nothing on its face seemed wrong with it. The Moons had lived beside the deserted house for some time.

The Moons were ludicrously well off and I heard a rumor that in an even more profitable time they had a narrow, closed off hallway where they placed various exotic animals, their heads poking through holes, so to those on the other side they looked like living taxidermy. I have not seen such a hallway, but like I said, I'm not exactly a frequent visitor. Still, I doubt that's true.

Claudia was a great host. She told jokes that were actually something I could laugh at. She had become a truly funny person, as often happens to those who have experienced a certain degree of suffering. It was clear that Lincoln loved her murderously, which was refreshing with this type of crowd.

It turns out I can pretend just enough to make it through one of these events. I've unfortunately been over-educated, but this was a case where it was helpful.

I got stuck in only one mock-scholarly conversation. People were discussing justice on a philosophical level; retributive, distributive and so forth. I tried to define it internally while others droned on. All I could think about were the crumbs and lint I find on my couch that I shove underneath the cushions every time I get up. How I imagine the lint and crumbs accumulating, swirling into a round ball until it becomes a giant, angry lint monster artlessly lumbering toward me. And that, to me, is justice. That makes sense.

"Is Bianca here?" I asked a few people huddled in the corners of the main room and hallway. Most were unresponsive. A girl who looked suspiciously too young to be holding two martini glasses pointed across the room with a full hand and simply replied, "Her friend Isabelle," then closed her eyes briefly.

*

3. A wasp desperately beating against a sun-filled skylight.

Isabelle turned out be be rather helpful. She told me Bianca was staying with a new boyfriend close to the center of town.

I stopped at a deli on MacCorkle on the way, figuring a full stomach would take some of the desperation out of my eyes.

A bearded guy answered the door and didn't seem overly concerned that a stranger was on his stoop. He invited me in with one swift motion. Maybe I looked like someone's father. I was.

We passed through the kitchen where bananas were laid out on the counter in various stages of decay. Light streamed in from the oversized windows and skylights. It looked like several people lived here.

He handed me a mug of what appeared to be coffee and got out another mug for himself.

"Does Bianca live here?" I asked, afraid of breaking the spell by speaking.

He nodded multiple times until it lost its meaning.

"She does," the steam rose from his mug in the midst of his pause as if to emphasize his words, "but she left. Went to see her aunt out in Ashland. Lives in a big house by the Army Navy store."

I sipped at the coffee. He didn't even ask who I was or why I wanted to find her. It was as if people came around looking for her all the time. Hell, I was looking for this girl and I didn't even know her.

I thanked him, patted his shoulder firmly a few times for his willingness to help and got on the road. I drove west for a while and it grew dark. I passed an oil refinery with millions of tiny flames flickering in the empty night. It was both stunning and industrial and I marveled at how it could be both.

An old, used-up air freshener in the shape of a leaf swung from side to side on my rearview mirror as I exited the highway.

I pictured the aunt's house even though I had no address and had clearly never visited before. I was actually picturing my middle school best friend's house. My brain has a reel that plays memories endlessly. They're seemingly of no significance or relevance to my current experience. I still find them comforting but I think only because they are from the past, not because of their content. I'm not sure if this is what happens before those memories burst and finally dissipate, a last show of sorts, because the pathetic flood of them is too overwhelming to discern. It gets to the point where I can't hear a lecture or read a story without imagining the plot played out in the context of one of these memories. My grandparents' patio. My first grade class-room. What I'm supposed to conclude from this, what my brain is compulsively, perhaps helplessly, attempting to portray, I can't grasp.

It started after my first robbery. I didn't even need to pull out the gun. It was just implied. It felt warm in my back pocket though it wasn't. I could have been faking. It felt like I was.

I circled past the Army Navy store and spotted a few nice homes to try.

What kind of trouble was this Bianca girl in?

Why was her mother looking for her?

Why couldn't her mother find her? It seemed easy enough.

A woman in her very early twenties sat on a front porch, smoking. This had to be Bianca. She had to be in some kind of trouble. She had to be waiting to be rescued.

I turned off the engine and opened the car door. Then I immediately closed it and started up the car again, because what am I doing thinking I was anything better?

Criminal

You were thinking that your car's air conditioner smelled like wet gravel when your sister-in-law called. The smell concerned you. It made you think the car was filling with fumes that would breed little polyps in your brain, your blood vessels, all the invisible places in your body. You let your phone ring, feigning safety at the wheel. But you immediately called her back once you arrived home.

She told you that your older brother, her husband of eleven years, the father of her two toddlered and tottering children, had been arrested. As in the police handcuffed him and put him in a stale, colorless room somewhere.

She told you why: he had stolen from a convenience store. When confronted, he had brutally beaten the employee behind the counter. She told you it was one of those coffee shop/gas station/deli counter/trucker bath-house-type places that jammed everything together in one incongruous chain but, as promised, was rather convenient. She thought you wanted to know these things.

These words sounded wrong. Like hearing wind chimes tinkling on your neighbor's porch in the middle of the night when you can't sleep. This could not be your brother. Your brother did not do these types of things. You thought it was a joke but this wasn't her kind of humor. You swallowed your saliva and it came back up, your throat like a clogged drain.

He stole chips. A couple of bags of chips, some pretzels maybe, some bottles of water charged with neon vitamins. He had money. He could have afforded to buy these items. Every bag, all the bags. Maybe the store itself if Ryan didn't need braces next year.

You apologized to your stunned sister-in-law, though you weren't sure why. She was the one who disrupted your reality. You apologized and it was like offering her a wayward piece of gum you found at the bottom of your purse.

Fascination welled up in you along with disgust. You were beginning to believe those reactions could not exist without the other. You thought about the bags of chips. You imagined, like all good food packaging, the bags boasted about all the harmful ingredients they didn't include rather than the ones they did. No trans-fats. No saturated fats. All zeros in a line.

*

You were still young. For the past few years, you were figuring out how to have an adult life, what that consisted of exactly. So far, you found that you had to try out a few fake ones first, really get your bearings. You probably didn't make any sense at the time and people had to be patient with you. They had to not laugh condescendingly at your lack of life, those mercurial series of selves. But sometimes you still felt the shame as if they did laugh, the heat of their eyes on you. This inchoate discovery was happening while your brother was busy having babies, putting others first. He didn't have the luxury of overthinking his identity until it gave him migraines.

Your brother, Hunter. You always called him Aggie, mostly because your mother called him that when she was in her affectionate moods. You didn't know where this nickname came from or what it meant. You asked your mother all the time and she just shrugged as if she couldn't remember or didn't know either. Aggie brought home second prize in the science fair; Hunter James put gum in his sister's hair. He was always Aggie to you. Your brother's world was now PTA meetings, eBay ratings, first aid kits in the glove compartments of both cars.

When you were in the third grade, you took Aggie and your friend Sarah through the woods to show them the hole in the ground packed with baby bunnies. Sarah slid in the mud and hit her head on a rock on the way down. You learned how much heads bleed. How they can flow more steadily than the creek near the bunny hole. How when you see blood you slip into a state of paralysis; how you didn't have a word for this state at that point. How Aggie is the opposite of you. He tore off the bottom of his shirt and wrapped up her head tightly. He carried her like a new bride over to the neighbors' house while you stared at his newly exposed bellybutton shaped in a perfectly round circle. On the way home, you clung to his arm like a rail on a listing ship.

*

Your brother's wife, though currently (and under-standably) bedraggled, looked like a sitcom character whose name you couldn't bring to the front of your brain, but wasn't interesting enough to act like her. She was more like a forgotten sleeve of saltines in the back of the pantry.

You agreed to meet her at the park mid-way between your respective neighborhoods. It had been raining or snowing or sleeting for five days straight, so you brought your umbrella. She complimented you on it. You volleyed with noticing her new haircut. This was talk to distract from what you should have been talking about.

You both strolled in a loop around a large man-made lake in the park where chivalrous, retired men liked to go fishing. Someone at the park must keep it stocked with some kind of fish.

Your brother's wife said the kids were staying at her parents' house in Cincinnati for a few weeks until things were "sorted out." She was doing what she must have thought your brother wanted her to do. As if he were dead. You wondered how much they were talking, if that one phone call thing was real or a cinematic fabrication. You had never needed to know before. You walked her to her car, still holding up the umbrella underneath both of you even though there was nothing to shield yourselves from anymore. The sleet had stopped a few minutes earlier.

She lingered at her car door. She was taking her time because there was no need to rush back to no one. There was a kind of freedom and stillness in her sadness. A catching of breath, if somewhat fragmentary.

You pictured the house she was returning to, riddled with toys and papers but organized in tidy piles. Your brother's homemade kombucha forming in the glass jar on the top of their fridge like a dead jellyfish floating to the surface of the polluted sea. Yet imbued with health, if you could get past its graphic origins.

He had many hobbies. He collected vintage cartoon lunch boxes that were rather valuable. But it made you think about the in-between years, how he had to love those lunch boxes when most people were getting rid of them, when they were worthless. How he had existed in that uncomfortable lapse of appreciation.

*

In one of those aforementioned affectionate moods, your mother would watch you and your brother roughhouse on the scratchy living room carpet and call you "Two peas in a pod." You misheard her, not knowing the expression. "Two PEES in a POT?!" you shrieked with glee, glancing almost murderously at your brother.

That year, you insisted that your name was Trixie, though it was not and is not. You wanted to be named after your favorite girl detective from those extra pulpy paperbacks you checked out at the library. The pages smelled like an old sweater locked away in a cedar chest. The books were so old they were no longer even yellowed but browned, as if returning to their arboreal nature. You always found them on the lazy susan racks at the end of the aisle. The metal racks coated in a thick, gummy plastic. Susan: now that's a name you didn't want.

*

Your brother was incarcerated. The convenience store employee was inconveniently lingering in the hospital with some internal bleeding. You couldn't remember what time of year it was. The date was vague and indistinguishable. Then you kept seeing fish sandwich deals on television and you knew it must be around Lent. People strictly adhering to rules in which they no longer believed for the sake of comfort that comes from familiarity.

The precipitous skies darkened the day outside your window and then strangely brightened the night. The glistening whiteness of snow paralleled the wall of clouds above until they were a seamless entity. The night just as bright, just as dark, as the day.

Recovery

It was waiting for her just inside her front door. It was in the corner, thinking it could go by unnoticed. But somehow she saw it anyway, right when she dropped her keys on the little table that she liked to throw things that were in her hands, things from the outside world she no longer wanted to touch now that she was inside.

Ingrid wanted all spiders to be dead, especially this one in the corner, but she didn't like killing them. This was both frustrating and relieving, as it was rumored that in her extended family there existed at one point in time a real, actual cannibal. It made her feel like the blood inside her body was capable of anything. But then there was this kind of moment, feeling something like relief, where she couldn't stand the feeling of an exoskeleton crushed against her hand, even with a paper towel in between.

She used to be more courageous.

The abduction had occurred five years ago. It only lasted three hours. Three hours of her life. It didn't seem like it should permeate the rest of the years the way that it had, such a small number of hours. She had escaped the man. The man who was poorly equipped for abduction and who was too nervous to ultimately decide on much of anything except keeping her trapped in a car going a moderate speed on an interstate for three hours. He was thin, white, sweaty; everything you would expect in an abductor.

Now, when considering backing out of plans, feeling constrained, she stopped because she couldn't find a suitable reason. Her friends would have parents in the hospital, sick children. What could she say was the matter? Could she say she was paralyzed? Could she say she was unable to catch up to the moment she was already in? You could miss a whole life this way, just trying to catch up to it. Couldn't you?

She carried a switchblade in her purse, in the hidden zipper pocket nestled beside her mini hot sauce bottle. She would carry the switchblade in her purse for the next seven months, unfailingly.

*

Ingrid worked for a local university in a town so small, the sign insisted on putting "historic downtown" in front of its name as if attempting to sell itself. She liked to walk around campus after work and find the apocalyptic street preacher. She was the only one who ever engaged him in conversation. When he would warn passersby about the approaching end of the world with great petulant shouts she would ask him questions. Things like, "Didn't it already end a while ago?" or "If you could gather all of the world's old, unused pay phone booths, what would you do with them? Put them in a museum next to the T-Rex exhibit?" She liked the feeling of being ignored by the only person that everyone else ignored.

The campus was abuzz with students constantly; students languorously sauntering down the labyrinthine pathways. Sometimes the pathways were too winding and not direct enough when one was already late for class, so the students would wear straight lines through the otherwise pristine lawns until the lines were entirely trampled dirt, to the vexation of the campus landscaping staff.

The students' faces would run together on her walks and she enjoyed imagining they were all the same chirping faces, an exuberant community of cacophony. It didn't seem like it was all that long ago that she was a college student. She distinctly remembered an introductory biology class where her professor described a miscarriage in full detail. He was gentle about it in some ways but still unrelenting about the specifics. A girl got up to leave in the middle of the lecture and fainted as she was swinging open the classroom door. Ingrid couldn't blame the girl. She often thought about circulatory systems, respiratory systems, other bodily systems, breathing that is constant and necessary to sustaining life, everything so vulnerable. Humans are too breakable to be real.

She thought about this breakability again when she received a call from some saintly hospital's nurse and was told that her grandmother had had a stroke. She was doing fine, considering the circumstances.

*

Driving back into her hometown, she watched people in their yards along the main roads. People watering their lawns, tending to plants, looking so settled and lived-in, confident and slow in their movements. As if they knew a secret about living here and that's why they could feel so good about living out their days here. But Ingrid had lived here before and it wasn't like that for her. She had not felt this way.

Her grandma was still in the hospital but was being sent home soon. She would go to an outpatient facility for rehabilitation three days per week. That was the plan. Ingrid didn't think she looked much different than usual when she saw her lying in the hospital bed, her skin maybe a little more sallow.

"I'm sorry, this is terrible. How are you?"

Her grandma shrugged. "I'm okay. It's not so bad. A little frustrating. But I got struck by lightning once and became a more eloquent speaker. And I won a small pot of money from a scratch-off ticket but my friends borrowed it all away until I had less money than before. So who knows what's good for me? I don't. This could be my big break."

She gave her grandma's hand a gentle squeeze, navigating the tubes. A man walked in. He had the look of a man who used to be pudgy and had lost weight too quickly. His stomach hung as if it were melting into a puddle and his face was very narrow, the cheekbones and jawline defined.

"I'm Max. You must be Ingrid."

He immediately went into a spiel about how stroke rehab doesn't cure stroke effects since it can't reverse brain damage, but that there are a lot of skills that can be relearned. It sounded like he was reading off a teleprompter on the wall behind her head. He relaxed a little and continued, "It's just muscle memory. Like learning how to play the guitar or swim. We're just glad she has her language abilities. Those were untouched. That's a big deal. Right, Ms. Beacon?"

She grunted in response.

"We'll be working on grasping objects and relieving pain in her limbs. Plus, we'll give her a little something for the sleep disturbances for a bit, just to get things moving in the right direction," said Max.

Ingrid didn't like the sound of sleep disturbances but she didn't really want to ask what that entailed.

*

Ingrid stayed at her grandma's house without her grandma there. She spent most of her time drinking tea in the most sunlit room of the house in the afternoons. It was also the most dilapidated of the rooms, with a framed picture of a stately castle hung directly above a large crack in the plaster that ran to the ceiling. It spoke equally to her grandma's sense of hope and sense of irony.

A clock ticked in this room, which was unnerving to Ingrid at first because who used real clocks anymore? The florid pattern of the couch reminded her of sitting here in elementary school reading mystery chapter books. Her grandma caught her smelling the pages of her book once, something she did almost every page turn because it was part of the experience of reading. The pleasant, pulpy scent.

Her grandma looked rather concerned and said, "Your face is so close to your book. Do you need glasses?" Ingrid shook her head furiously from side to side, too embarrassed to explain herself. For the rest of the day, she went back to reading without smelling the pages and her book lost a dimension.

Ingrid noticed the stereotypical knitting needles neatly piled on top of the books and magazines on the end table by the couch, the canvas tote bag filled with yarn on the floor beside it. Her grandma was always knitting baby blankets. Even if she didn't know anyone having a baby, she kept at it. She alternated between blue and pink yarn. She always found someone to use the blankets. Things were always continuing, somehow.

*

Her grandma was being released from the hospital. She could barely grip well enough to pull herself out of the bed, but supposedly she had been there long enough.

"You know, this woman I used to work with, every time she was feeling down, she would buy one of those tank tops that say 'Bride' in cursive rhinestones across the chest and wear it around just so she could get smiles and romantic looks from strangers. Should we try that tactic for you, too?" Ingrid asked.

"How do you know I don't already receive my fill of romantic looks?"

"Good point."

This comment made Ingrid think about when her grandma had tried to set her up with an accountant named Buck. Buck's hair was thinning and he looked constantly startled. They had eaten a spaghetti dinner on his front porch. He had stuck a candlestick in a two liter pop bottle in the middle of the table. Throughout the meal, she thought of the time her neighbor asked her to watch her parakeet while she went to South America. The parakeet was covered in pink, wrinkly tumors. They pushed out from under his feathers unapologetically. It was hard to look at him, knowing he would die as soon as her neighbor boarded the plane.

"Let's take you home," Ingrid said, handing over the paperwork to a nurse.

*

Returning back to her small university town, she took a walk and found the street preacher ranting on his favorite corner.

Ingrid asked him, "Why is this moment always going to be better when I remember it than it is right now?"

He just kept right on going.

The Fire

4:07am, February 10, 5572 Fairbrook Ave.

The fire started at Ms. Mary Comstock's house. Mary was old, so old she couldn't hear worth a damn. She always watched her movies on mute, studying the overly expressive faces as if they had lost the power to speak and could only mouth words soundlessly in order to communicate. It made her feel like she had some sort of power over them.

Her deafness also meant that she certainly didn't hear the cracks and pops of her furniture, let alone the roar of the fire, when she was deeply asleep. She didn't even feel the menacing smoke as it smothered her crow-footed face, as it passed over her spotted hands with veins like long, blue ropes strung up underneath her skin.

If she could have heard all the popping noises as her house was consumed in flames, it would have reminded her of the pops of her canning jars back when she used to pickle vegetables from her garden. Back when she had a garden.

The fire had started due to an overloaded electrical socket in her living room. It was February and her Christmas tree, months old, was still next to the socket because who would know? Who would see? Because from where was she supposed to draw the strength it would take to remove it? The only reason she even had a Christmas tree was because her son said he would visit on Christmas Day. He was forty-four years old but was adamant about his mother keeping everything exactly the same as he remembered it. She had taken a few posters down from his old bedroom years earlier and he had stormed out of the house in disappointment. So she tried to keep things as similar to how they were when he was a child, just to please him.

The very real Christmas tree had become very dry and pyrolyzed in the flames, creating a wall of gray smoke against the black smoke that had already accumulated.

*

5:00pm, February 9, 5574 Fairbrook Ave.

Britta James liked to sit under the kitchen skylight with her mug of coffee and let the gray winter light reflect off the surface of it like mercury while she waited for her husband to come home.

This particular day, Britta thought about how she and Wheeler used to go to a nearby vineyard in the summers, lay on the lawn and talk about the days feeling both long and short at the same time. She thought about how they didn't do that anymore. *But we don't not do it, it's just too cold for the vineyard, it's still winter*, she told herself, shaking her head. She only spoke in double negatives when she was sleep deprived.

Britta was a freelance handwriting expert. Her job was becoming obsolete. She thought about her role as a movie premise: A not-so-young woman is able to interpret every idiosyncratic wisp of pen but is unable to interpret basic human behaviors, such as love and the expression of it. Her stomach curdled at the fact that she was able to come up with such a trite summary.

Britta was worried that Wheeler would not come home tonight. She let the mug warm the tips of her fingers. She wondered if she should move out, move to that downtown condo; the tingle of homeownership without all the hedge trimming.

But Britta and Wheeler James would end up staying the night together, together with the rest of their cul-de-sac neighbors, very soon, on the floor of the local elementary school gym. She would experience the horror of fluorescent lights, the porous, flimsy look of the cinderblock walls painted white, the racing stripes in the school's colors (blue and gold) along the sides of the wall in a flourish.

*

2:35pm, February 8, 5573 Fairbrook Ave.

Wheeler James rapped respectfully on the front door of Mr. Cornelius Starling's home. He grew impatient on the stoop. Feeling mutinous, he thought about running away before Corny could reach the door, the trek over here Britta's weak attempt at fostering neighborly community.

But Corny reached the door, not exactly clambering to get there, more like shuffling. Wheeler was welcomed inside the sweltering house. Corny kept the temperature up high and the humidifier running almost constantly. He kept it so hot and dank in there, and his front hallway was so narrow, that stepping into it felt like stepping into an esophagus. Constellations of lint were gathered on the carpet.

Corny always had a toothpick dangling from the right side of his mouth, and when he would later hear of Ms. Mary Comstock's death, he would weep like an embarrassed child being bullied on the playground.

"Mr. Starling, we were – I was wondering if you'd like me to – while I already have the snow shovel out, just take care of your driveway, too? I mean, just to make things easier," said Wheeler. *Why do I sound so exasperated?* he thought.

Corny just sniffed, pushed out his toothpick a little more so that it dangled from his lips.

"It's not that I think you need help or anything. Your yard always looks so pristine," said Wheeler. It was the perfect amount of true. True enough to be flattering but not so true that it made them uncomfortable.

"Sure," Corny grunted, "go ahead." He waved his hand back and forth and Wheeler wasn't sure if the wave was in dismissal or encouragement. Talking to him reminded Wheeler of a famous head coach who always gave an abbreviated explanation to sideline reporters before running decidedly in the opposite direction.

Wheeler smiled and made his way quickly back through the digestive tract of hallway.

Cornelius Starling had become somewhat of an amateur ornithologist. He had always wanted to bird watch but didn't want to appear narcissistic due to his last name, so he held off until retirement. His binoculars had a thin film of dried grease where his face pressed against them as he observed the *turdus migratorius* flit around his stone birdbath in the backyard.

*

4:16am, February 10, 5574 Fairbrook Ave.

It had begun to snow as the fire reached the outer wall of Britta and Wheeler James' house. The outside temperature had been quickly dropping through the night; the fire, fueled by manufactured materials, as if some twisted answer to prayer for warmth. The hard freeze had slowed down the molecules, slowing down the minutes before the fire along with it, as Britta stared, awake in bed. The night as cold and vast as its sky. She shivered under the quilt and studied the deadly peace of the black stillness. Even the frames on their wall had been affected by the snowstorm; the temperature constricting the walls and the frames sliding crookedly in complaint.

Then she heard cracking, felt choked for oxygen, wondered if she was having a panic attack. She tasted the fire before she saw it.

Choking, she shook Wheeler awake before even thinking of whether she really wanted to. They held hands as they navigated what used to be a recognizable floor plan. The fire was turning their home into a newly discovered planet, scorched and uninhabitable.

"Where are we?"

"Where are we?"

"Where are we?"

Wheeler kept asking through his coughs.

"Shh," Britta said, leading him out the front door after testing that it was cold enough to open.

By the time they curled up in the street next to the snow drifts, jacketless and bewildered, the fire trucks were attempting to make the tight turn of the cul-de-sac circle. Corny had called the firemen, had somehow managed to grab his down vest and binoculars before escaping, and was spitting into the snow as he waited.

They stood and watched because what else could they do? They stood and watched because they were powerless against the flames. But not completely powerless, because they were alive. And wasn't being alive remarkable?

The three of them were pretty dazed from the smoke trying to invade their lungs and head. Britta found herself thinking of her grandfather, the conversation they had when her other grandfather had died. He had told her she would start seeing his face in strangers, be reminded of him everywhere. He had said this with such confidence but she wasn't convinced. Her mother's father was so distinct looking, there was no way anyone else could look like him. He ended up not only being exactly right in his prediction, but this conversation also happened to be one of their last, as if he were preparing her for his own death, too. Britta wondered if the same principles could be true for houses that were destroyed.

"Where's Ms. Comstock?" Corny shouted at her. The fire truck's water began to freeze after being released from the hose and some of the uniformed men started to slip and fall on the pathway to the Comstock residence.

*

4:28am, February 10, 5575 Fairbrook Ave.

Clarence Egerton lived in the same small cul-de-sac made up of new homes fully constructed of composite wood.

Clarence's house was shrouded in black smoke, the manufactured wood like a gallon of gasoline to the fire that had spread from Ms. Mary Comstock's house. Clarence was completely unaware of the fire, as he was in Cancun, Mexico at a flea market, with gritty sand naturally exfoliating his rough heels as he walked.

He didn't really know his neighbors very well, though he was often talked about. Clarence was the only crossing guard they knew who drove a BMW. They also had discovered he was a part-time nudist, as his curtains were rather sheer. Clarence stayed a mystery to them because they liked it that way, and he did too.

Compulsive Truths

You make stupid-good money as a Santa Claus. Sure, there are parents who scan you up and down for any trace of child molester and there are kids who spit on you. But you'd be surprised how many children are just ecstatic to meet a guy who brings them presents without asking for something in return.

I started the whole Santa Claus thing after my ribs were broken and I could no longer work construction. The cops still don't know where the person is who broke those ribs.

Here's how it all went down. I had just moved into my new house when someone knocked on the door a bit more vigorously than usual. It was a rather large guy with a dubious stance but I tried not to make any snap judgments.

"Is Frank in?" he asked.

I told him there wasn't any Frank who lived here.

He just scoffed. "I know Frank's here. I need to talk to him."

"Sorry. Wrong house," I said.

"If there's no one else here then you must be Frank."

I insisted that I wasn't Frank, that in fact my name was Lancaster, and he looked at me like, *that has to be a bullshit name*, and I couldn't really disagree with him there, but still I had to try. He stepped into the house.

Then he got physical. I can't remember the details but I know I couldn't see out of my right eye very well, that I was somehow lying on the floor, and that I desperately wanted to be someone named Frank just so I could reveal whatever information this guy needed.

"I'm not him, I swear," I heard myself saying while blood filtered from my nose into my mouth.

I've tried to develop my own theories since no one else seems to be. I couldn't get much from my landlord about the previous tenant, but I imagine that wall of a man really did have the wrong house. He might have been looking for the house diagonally across from mine. Too many people live there to know for sure.

These neighbors leave for weeks at a time, the house looking more depressed in its shabbiness when no one is there to enliven it. Then they return and have these large bonfires, dancing around the fire with great flaming torches, asquirm with hallucinogens, looking elaborate and exotic. They also like to dance around what I refer to as the maypole, but what is actually a large stake in the ground that they tied strips of old undershirts to.

They have names like Drake and Crystal and Heaven; names that reveal a lot about their parents.

*

Moving to this absurd block became a necessity when my wife divorced me. We had eloped when we weren't all that young and probably should have known better.

The first thing I noticed about Bridget was her hair. It was always stringy and pieced apart like a child's. Like if she tried to pull it up or contain it in some way it would just fall right back down.

I guess her hair reminded me of the woman who worked in the video store in town a decade or two ago. She was in her mid-30s with a glass eye, articulate and seemingly in her prime. Her light brown, crimped hair fell around the edges of her frames, the right lens purposefully clouded to hide what lay behind it.

I always wondered how someone like her could have ended up there, handing over chunky VHS tapes to kids with sticky hands. And I wondered how Bridget had ended up with me, too. On one of our first real dates I started rubbing her arm and she reciprocated, thinking I must find it comforting or I wouldn't have thought to do it. After a couple of minutes she noticed she was still rubbing my arm and I had long since stopped. This could be an accurate summary of our marriage.

Naturally, when things ended I fell into a bit of a slump. I knew I was no better and no less selfish than suicidal people. I had entitlement issues and some depressive spells occasionally, but the only thing that made me different was curiosity. I expected life to be shitty, but I was still curious about what that shittiness would look like. How it would play itself out.

Bridget now lives in a clean, suburban neighborhood with its own park. She has a very white house with all of the interior walls painted a very striking red. The contrast is intense, like an overly pale person is trying to consume you when you walk in.

*

Becoming Santa lifted me up out of the confusion of being both newly alone and mauled by a stranger within a few short months. Let's just say I already looked the part. I was a little nervous leaving the construction field, but after the assault, sitting in a comfortable chair wearing red pajamas was as big and sexy of an idea as the fear telling me not to do it.

I started in malls and switched to private parties and corporate events after I got smart.

There are training courses and conferences all over the country for those interested, but you can learn a lot just by staying alert on the job. I signed up for all the major toy store catalogs so I know what I'm talking about with the kids. You learn pretty early on that if they ask for a pony or something equally outrageous, you're supposed to say "I'll see what I can do," rather than making any promises.

Plus, beard-dyeing is actually tax-deductible.

Of course there are downsides, like anything. If you look like Santa and you're strolling along with hookers on each arm and a crack pipe in your mouth, and a young child happens to see you, who knows what will happen. Even if you're dressed in regular clothes, they can spot you. They know. So I've had to quit smoking because I don't want to be responsible for the youths of America keeling over from lung cancer.

After a particularly rough day of loud shrieking in my ear and urine, vomit or some other excretion from the human body soaking my suit, I open my toilet lid and search around for my emergency pack of cigs taped inside. And they look like cigarettes that one could simply smoke. I just crack a window.

*

Since becoming divorced I've attempted dating as a way of making it seem as though I'm putting myself out there. Dating is like seeing an object shining in the sun and leaning over to see it's only a penny but you're already leaned too far over to stop. As I went to see if it was worth it, I found out it was definitely not worth it.

Somehow I've become involved with this woman Delia who blows her nose exactly like how my uncle used to. It's very loud and boisterous but that just makes it seem that much more genuine, almost imploring in its sound. I say "involved with" because I think it sounds classier than just a plain old relationship.

Now my phone buzzes angrily against the wooden kitchen table, amplified by the hard surface. Now in my nostrils there is only the acrid burn of the processed sardines in her Caesar salad dressing. Now there is only insert sentiment here.

Delia and I met through Lenny, who is unfortunately one of the elves I call up frequently for Christmas parties. Lenny's glasses are always so noticeably smudged that I don't know how he stands it let alone how he can see. As if he not only accepted the results of the broken earth but embraced it. And what exactly is he doing to get them that way in the first place? Delia told me he's a compulsive liar who licks people's shoes in movie theaters and I believe it.

*

I asked a kid what he wanted for Christmas last December and he paused a long while, then sighed and said, "Just a decent night's sleep would be nice," and I thought, I don't think I've heard a better answer.

When actors break scene they have different rituals for transitioning out of character and back into themselves. I feel the need for that also. I like to remember that I'm not a bearded, overjoyed myth but a regular human male, and there's a relief in that I can't explain.

Too Much of the Wrong Thing

You had that feeling of forgetting something again. It struck you when trying to find a seat on the plane. That panicky feeling, sifting through all the filters in your mind for what that missing thing could be, coming up empty. You probably didn't forget anything; you'll just always be missing something you can't name.

It was difficult to leave. Your room framed the trees outside in full arabesque. Living in a hotel is sad but comforting. You love the feeling of uninhabited living spaces. The rooms are too blank to be a real home in their purgatorial, uncluttered way. Everyone lives there and no one lives there.

You didn't want anyone to sit next to you on the plane. You didn't want to explain that you were traveling to St. Louis for a routine eye exam. That's the kind of thing people use as an excuse for dismissing you. You didn't want to talk about your irrelevant town that is small and hollowed out, not sure how to come alive without reliving the past, paralyzed by its bountiful history. The only thing it has and the only thing holding it back.

A middle aged woman ended up sitting next to you. She reminded you of one of your teachers from high school. The teacher who played clips from *Dead Poets Society*, her taciturn admittal that the only way to inspire students was to learn from a teacher other than herself. One that was fictional was decidedly best.

The woman sitting next to you was manic in her conversation. It was almost more relieving than silence because her speech was so constant you knew you would never have to speak. *Mydaughterisincollegeandsheonly needsfifteenmorecreditstograduateearly* –

*

You felt like a banana on its tremulous journey home in a flimsy grocery bag. The chime on the door was piercing, the printer in the waiting room volcanic. A labeled chart of the eyeball was framed on the wall. It was shaded and color coded and it looked like a newly discovered planet. You waited. You wondered why people didn't say they were 'just feeling things' the way that they said they were 'just seeing things.'

You tried to be patient: it was a waiting room. The chair seemed skeletal, like it was an extra backbone: rather sharp and uncomfortable but you needed it for support. The air was humid with the sighs of others, fetid with the presence of so many bodies passing through.

You thought about the second grade. Your eyes were still growing and changing shape. You would visit the eye doctor just when you had grown comfortable with not seeing very well. The blur would sneak up on you. With your new prescription, the clouds were so crisp and defined, the leaves so veiny and precise, that it all seemed false.

That same year, your teacher made up an exercise about understanding blindness. He asked everyone what blind people see. What does nothingness look like? Blackness? Whiteness? No one had a satisfying answer. You imagined asking the question to a person who was born with sight and had gone blind. Maybe the imaginary person looked a little like Stevie Wonder, your favorite artist who happened to be blind. What does nothingness look like? you asked this imaginary blind person wearing sunglasses. You waited for the answer, staring at your reflection in their dark lenses.

Then the front desk person was calling your name and leading you down a hallway, asking you questions you thought were unnecessary and unrelated to your eye health.

*

When you met him, you treated him as any other guest. Because he was, at least at that point. You were covering the front desk because you had let people go the week before. It was right after you had tried your first night shift and you think it showed.

He strolled up, this dumpy man with this tall, gorgeous woman. The difference between them was almost comical. The woman held a leash that was clipped to a stately greyhound. He was surrounded by giants.

The woman and the dog were rather stunning and you found it challenging to focus on the man trying to meet your eyes. When yours irresolutely floated over to his, you noticed that a little sliver of his iris was missing, like someone had carved out a crescent of it. Bald and bold, he shook your hand. Or maybe he didn't shake your hand and it just felt like he did. You gave them keys to one of the pet-friendly rooms away from the elevator and watched the dog saunter away languorously.

*

The second time you saw him, the first time you really met him, was at your hotel bar. You were covering a bartending shift. You were embarrassed. You thought it looked like you were the only employee in this hotel. You basically were now. A person with an ice sculpting business was having a conversation with a locksmith. You thought how incredibly useful one's profession was in comparison to the other's.

"My dog never liked her anyway," the ice sculptor was saying.

The man approached the bar and chose a seat near the middle. He had his pick; the other two were the only ones at the bar. He ordered a whiskey, neat, and kept his eyes fixed on you.

"What brings you here?" you asked, looking down at the empty glass in your hand.

"My wife is speaking at an infectious disease conference," he said.

His wife would later add a PhD to her MD, studying the sociological effects of infectious disease. How major diseases reveal people's coping mechanisms: some people hearing news updates three or four times a day and immediately forgetting, others obsessed and paranoid to the point of illogical precautions, perseverating on the history and growth of the disease. After her dissertation was approved, his wife's brain would then quickly fade like a dying star, its energy wildly spent and ready to stop.

"Is the conference downtown?" you asked. You handed him the drink.

"Yes. At the convention center," he said.

"Then what are you doing all the way out here?" you asked. It sounded more accusatory than you would have liked.

"I wanted to meet you," he said.

The guys at the end of the bar were still occupying each other with full glasses of beer, so you leaned in and asked, "What do you mean?" You thought maybe he was trying to pick you up, that the beautiful wife was a cover.

"I was your uncle at one time. I was married to your aunt. Your father's sister," he said.

You thought of Aunt Maureen: the adventurous one in the family. She lived in Denver and used mineral-based makeup. She made her own scarves and sold them at the market. You saw her every eight years or so. She had been married approximately four times.

"So you're Mitchell? Or Steve?" you asked.

"Yes. Your Uncle Mitchell, I suppose. She got rid of me quick," he said, taking a sip.

"It seems like you've done pretty well for yourself without her," I said. It was nice that it happened to be true.

"I got lucky," he said.

You found out that he was an ophthalmologist, and when people called him an optometrist he corrected them by talking through his teeth. You also found out that he and his wife met as neighbors. She was half Korean and rather strict about people taking off their shoes at the front entrance. He knocked on her door one night and had to deliver the news that her cat was dead while looking at his wormy toes wiggling in his Gold Toe socks.

He was so flippant with all the details of his life that you felt you needed to reciprocate. You told him about the dying town that was making your hotel a dying hotel. You told him about how sometimes people leave interesting things in their rooms. Old guitars, a car door, sombreros, those inflatable neon stick figures that dance in the wind in front of stores. Things that stood for other things. You told him that often people accidentally leave little wads of powdery bills stuffed between the mattress and the box spring, that when things were slow, sometimes you checked before the maids came in, just in case.

It was only much later, in the middle of the night, when you realized what he was going to do. You had shared too much. Or maybe you had just shared too much of the wrong thing. You had sounded rather pitiful, you noticed too late. He could smell that you had no fallback plan.

When they checked out early the next morning, you found yourself in their room though you don't remember walking there. It was all there, enough to start over, or renovate the hotel, or move it closer to downtown, or just piss money away for a good long while. You weren't surprised but you wondered if he always carried that much cash around. If he already knew what he was going to do before he got here. He didn't have kids and he had plenty of means, you tried to justify. But it all felt utterly ridiculous.

*

He smiled at you and led you to the chair like you were just another patient. He inspected your eyes. You thought about how close his face gets to another person's face every day, several times a day. How intimate it would seem but how vacant it really was.

"You're nearsighted," he said.

"That's not the first time someone's accused me of that," you said.

You thought you should thank him or hug him or bring him a nice bottle of wine but nothing seemed right. Nothing seemed appropriate.

*

At the hotel bar, he had talked about retirement. He said he thought about it as death, that he always wanted to stay occupied and useful for as long as possible. You thought about how comfortable you were with relaxing. You could lay on the couch all day and it would feel nothing but pleasant. If you retired, you would just sit at a diner until close, watching people eat too fast and waitresses fill and refill coffees. You felt that being surrounded by the bustle would be enough.

Not My Place

They lived in a two-story house, with two different, but not all that different, stories. They were both named Charlotte; one named after the other by the one in between them.

The one in between them: the mother, the daughter, depending, used to house the older Charlotte, but it hadn't worked out so well. She hadn't been the best guardian. In her inescapable condition, the eldest Charlotte would put knives in the freezer or under the bed. The one in between them would watch and drink and laugh.

The youngest Charlotte needed something substantive to do so she didn't mind taking care of her grandmother. She had managed to find several jobs in the past decade despite her efforts to remain apathetic. She had once been a middle school English teacher but quit because grammar started to consume her. She began to think of people as punctuation. She thought of herself as a semicolon; always separate but desiring to be connected to something else. Her then-boyfriend as mysterious ellipses. Her mother as a walking exclamation mark.

To decompress, she earned a living solely by finding cats and dogs and other beloved pets with substantial rewards tied to them, unlike their leashes. The standard of living was low enough and the pet lovers were high enough to get by for a while that way. She found posters on the other side of town by the stately neighborhood on the hill to get the most out of her searches.

She relished in the time between finding the pets and giving them back. She loved to stare at the found dogs' nostrils; those perfectly inverted, calligraphic commas.

She was considering turning her house into a bed and breakfast before her mother called, but decided against it. Nothing blends intimacy and distance more than hosting strangers in your home.

Young Charlotte was relieved to take in her namesake. She was already constantly reminded of her. Her new house was near an old church that had working church bells. She found this quaint, but more than that. The bells chimed the same tune as her grandmother's clock she heard as a child, which rang out during their visits in the old living room, amid the seemingly endless conversation, the expensive dust collectors gleaming, asking to be touched, not allowed to be touched.

Plus, young Charlotte was lonely. The boyfriend was gone and good riddance to him. He had treated her like mailing tape: something transparent, something that should always be around if he needed it, but something he should never have to buy.

*

The eldest Charlotte settled in easily, her belongings pared down to a few boxes and a leather suitcase that had once been rather sophisticated. She would mostly lie in her bed or wander around the yard with vacant eyes. She would come in for supper and with her blood sugar rising, she would become chatty. She would talk about events from years ago, but with a ferocity that always convinced the younger that it had just occurred.

"I lost a tooth," she proclaimed one day, and the younger poked her fingers frantically around in the elder's mouth, searching for a hole.

"The tooth fairy even came," she continued, displaying her fully stocked grin.

Occasionally she would bring up selfless acts of valor, like tending to soldiers and putting back limbs where they belonged when she was a nurse during the war. Young Charlotte let her boast away. She didn't know anyone else who could tell these types of stories anymore and still be telling the truth.

Some of these dinnertime confessions were current, but only a few. She admitted to having a scandalous dream about their thirty-something neighbor, even flushed red a few times when he waved to her on his return home from work. But this only lasted a few weeks and then she barely acknowledged him. She became like the slow child a few houses down, simply a repetitive loudspeaker of common expressions.

Both Charlottes would often hear the distant echo of an ice cream truck in the evenings and believe its chimes haunting, almost discordant. Both Charlottes would look out the window, waiting to see it roll down the street but find nothing.

*

Young Charlotte awoke one morning and fumbled to the kitchen to start the coffee. The other Charlotte was not in her bed and had left it primly tucked and folded.

She checked the backyard, her favorite spot by the fence where she usually sat on a deck chair with her hands folded in her lap. But she was not there either.

When she didn't return after lunch, young Charlotte thought she'd better put on some pants. She called the police. While waiting on them, she knocked on the cute neighbor's door and asked, just in case. She did not call her mother. Not right away.

The cops asked her a few questions and tried to withhold their knowing glances. One asked her what her phone number was. She forgot, or chose to forget, and then forgot that she chose, and stuttered out the digits while looking out the window.

*

She attempted to fall asleep that night. A bird sounded off in the darkness with its high whistle.

"You are confused," she said to the bird, she said to her grandma, she said to herself.

She watched the local news the next day, something she usually never did. The reporter mentioned that a woman had delivered a baby yesterday without knowing that she was pregnant. Perhaps there was already a mass in her midsection, so maybe she didn't see the signs. Charlotte wondered how that was possible. Charlotte thought even in dire circumstances, people were still navigating life. Like they knew what life was and what it entailed.

She called her mother. Her mother became furious, worried, distraught, and selfishly, left out. Once again, her mother was left out of the family conversation. Her mother forgot that this cycle of dynamics proved, no matter how infuriating, that she was indeed part of the family.

*

A month later, nobody knew anything. Charlotte opened the door to the elder Charlotte's room and found the leather suitcase on the top shelf of her closet looking shockingly empty. She buried it in the backyard the way that it was, just to have buried something.

She hated herself for wondering, but she wondered what the neighbors thought as she dug the hole. She hoped they knew and hoped they didn't know at the same time.

That

She heard a crash outside. She looked out the window to be sure everything was how she left it. But it was night and the lamp was right next to the window so she could only see a vague form of herself glaring back. She had a surprisingly intimidating glare and was somehow impressed with it, forgetting all about the noise.

*

They met for a drink the next night. She couldn't even look him in the eyes without accumulating what resembled a late August sunburn. He was good. Too good.

He was too good and she thought of herself as a catfish. Catfish smelled like fish but weren't even nutritious like the other fish. Plus the name suggested they weren't sure whether they should be on land or in water. She thought if she acquired enough bumper stickers and tattoos, someone would take a large 1990s label maker to her forehead and she wouldn't have to wonder anymore.

She was early and sat in the parking lot of the bar. She

turned off the engine. She should have kept the car running just in case. But he managed to arrive.

Everything tasted either too watered down or over-salted. His favorite. She thought he would bring up California. But California was said in stares.

Every time she talked to him, her mouth made these impossibly, horribly embarrassing noises she had never made while talking to anyone else. Like the sounds her old Volvo made while in reverse. He was at least polite enough to pretend they didn't happen. But perhaps that was the problem: ignoring came too easy for him.

She noticed he was texting another friend, "I'm with Rhea," but auto-correct changed her name to "That" instead.

"I have to go," she heard herself saying.

*

As a child, on one of her first road trips, her mother handed her an apple from the front passenger seat. The juxtaposed crunchy outside and fleshy inside fascinated her. She didn't know not to consume it all because she had never experienced a whole, unattended apple. Her mother reached her hand back for the core and Rhea gave her a high five.

*

She didn't decide to stay in Pittsburgh after graduation but she didn't leave either. She had grown so used to the terrain; the hills on top of other hills. The South Side Slopes. Looking out on Mount Washington at the three rivers. To her, they always seemed like two rivers turning into one rather than three distinct rivers. One river always looked more brown and polluted, but they swirled and collapsed into each other as if they didn't really have a choice.

The land of tunnels. She used to try to hold her breath all the way through, her sister showing her how. You had to wait until the car was through to the other side. She would wait, wait for that speck of natural light instead of those orange stripes of fluorescent light lining the tunnel walls. Then she knew she might have a chance at winning. But who was there to beat? Herself? The Squirrel Hill Tunnel? She used to imagine herds of irritated squirrels burrowing through mounds of rock to make the tunnel, not knowing yet how things were named. But maybe she still doesn't.

*

He was supposed to meet her at the art museum, but she found herself in the middle of a conversation with an elderly man, clearly retired, who decided the best way to spend his remaining days was highlighting the major works of Abstract Expressionism.

The old man was laughing and fiddling with his bowtie. Then he smoothed his nonexistent hair. She assumed he still wasn't used to it being gone.

"If only we humans could communicate as well as animals," he concluded, apparently summing up whatever it was they were discussing.

"You know, I can't tell the difference between what I've said and what I've thought, and I certainly can't tell what I've fantasized becoming reality and what actually has."

All she had to contribute was honesty since she hadn't been listening.

*

She visited the quaint used bookstore. She had an affinity for buying books with others' names scrawled on the inside cover as a way of receiving a controlled portion of intimacy. Underlines and extra notes were like bonus points.

*

She thought of him as a trench coat. Historically, the trench coat went from professional to provocative to preppy. At least it got to be dynamic, she thought. Some coats are just coats. Parkas will always be parkas. But if she thought about it, trenchcoats were really only intended for the rain.

*

He called when she was asleep and she pretended that she was sneaking away at a party, as if the gravel in her throat wasn't there. He wanted her to come over.

"Come on, Rhea," he said in his buttery voice.

"Have you done radio before?" she asked.

"What?" he asked, then hung up right away.

She drove over, though it took her a while. East Carson Street didn't allow for people to turn left successfully, she thought. Or said?

She shared with him a poem she had written before she nodded off earlier that night:

I've been told a thousand times,

The difference between alligators and crocodiles,

But I don't think I'll ever remember

Until my leg gets bitten off by something in a swamp.

She knew it was a risk to share. She loved sharing too much. When she finished reciting, she received no response except the glare from his bright yellow wall.

It was very yellow. They would live in very yellow.

She was by his front door. He joked about next Tuesday and they laughed and she looked up and it was next Tuesday.

*

In second grade, she got into an argument with her best friend David because he wouldn't believe her that her grandma's first name was actually Grandma. She knew it sounded crazy but still resented that David didn't trust her, even more when he didn't speak to her the next day. "But really," she insisted.

*

She decided to start walking to his house late at night to avoid turning left at the light. Pittsburgh: the city who knew what it was like to boom with industry and success until the industry blackened the day to night and outsourced everything over to Japan. It knew emptiness, ghosts, great cost. The rebuilding process, much like anything useful, was taking far too long.

Erase

Graham enters the cinderblock one-story building for the fifth time this month. The month is December and everything is gray. Gray skies and gray snow. Graham finds all the gray comforting in its consistency.

He walks to a semicircular structure to prevent those entering the building from going any further without first stopping here to identify themselves. Graham tells the woman at this desk that he is here to see James Humboldt. "My..." unsure of how to say for several infinite seconds until he recalls the word, "... my ... f-father."

The woman nods from below the semicircle, remaining seated in a stained computer chair covered in what looks like dog fur. She nods from the great chasm that is below the top tier of the desk, tells him to have a seat.

Graham sits in a short row of chairs across from the reception desk and waits. Dr. Blaze meets him at the front, though he is unsure of whether Dr. Blaze intended to run into Graham or if he accidentally did on his way to another wing of the building. Regardless, Dr. Blaze escorts him down the hall to the left.

He notices how clean the floors are, how shiny and impeccable, while everything else appears stained or marred in some way. Even Dr. Blaze's white coat and dress pants are rumpled. The fluorescent lights reflect back to themselves through the gleaming floor as the two walk to Graham's father's room.

James is seated with a remote in one hand and his other hand draped delicately across his crotch. Like a ballerina's hand, Graham thinks. Each time he visits, his father has the remote grasped tightly in his hand even if he's not watching TV. He's not exactly sure, but it looked like during the last visit, his father covertly pressed the mute button while Graham was talking.

The facility lets James keep his dog in the room, which is nice. The brochure boasts its "pet-friendly atmosphere." Graham doesn't know what to think of his father's dog. It looks like a stuffed animal dog. Its name is Muffin, which sounds ridiculous to Graham. Muffin's great, round, black eyes are so unnaturally large that Graham has to look closely to convince himself they are not marbles, and even then it is questionable. Pieced out sections of fur cover the rest of it; fur that never quite comes together again, just like a well-handled toy.

Muffin is curled up next to James looking sullen, ossified into position. Dr. Blaze talks enthusiastically about Graham's father's current condition, flipping through some rudimentary handwritten notes. This impresses Graham. A personal touch. Dr. Blaze flips quickly through the notes but Graham catches something that looks like "given to laconic moods" in a lank, choppy script.

The doctor and James interact and start laughing about some incident with another resident, something that must be rather amusing, something they refer to as "the scandal" but what must be something much less intense. Graham shifts his weight through this conversation from foot to foot while the other men talk, having to go to the bathroom suddenly but feeling the need to stay, knowing he should wait until it is over without really knowing why.

Dr. Blaze pats James on the shoulder and walks out. For the rest of the visit, Graham and James watch an old sitcom and look at each other's feet while they talk during the commercials. So many questions bubble up in Graham but he suppresses them by sipping coffee from a shockingly white styrofoam cup.

As Graham leaves, he overhears a woman say to another woman right outside the main doors, smoking together, "I figured my sanity was more valuable than that jar of organic mayonnaise."

*

Earlier that month, when Delia called to tell him the news, Graham knew to pick up the phone because she rarely called. She had sounded perplexed even though she was the one relaying the news.

"They found Dad..." she started, and he could picture her moony, pregnant face swollen even more from tears. Graham expected from that half-statement to hear that they had found him dead. But she continued, "He ... he was in something called a dissociative fugue state. A *protracted* dissociative fugue state. Whatever the hell that is. I think it was on a Lifetime movie once. I didn't think this stuff was actually real."

Graham wasn't sure how to respond so he grunted in what he hoped was a sympathetic way.

"They found him in one of those traveling government work programs. He hadn't made it very far, just Morgantown. You know, the kind of program that goes door-to-door selling magazines. They get to ride around in buses all over the country with crumpled lists of magazines in their pockets trying to get people excited about subscriptions. It's pathetic," she sighed.

Graham knew the kind. He could tell they were legitimate if they seemed illegitimate.

"Anyway, he ended up somehow convincing some rich widower to let him live with her. He was just at her door trying to sell magazines but somehow he managed that. I don't really think they know all the details yet but they know her name and she used to work for the paper up here. Maybe you know her."

Graham tried to picture an old widower until he remembered a young, attractive Executive Editor whose husband had died tragically a year or two ago. She had moved to West Virginia after his death and supposedly lived on a large estate with exotic animals. That must be her, he thought.

He remembered seeing her only once at a party hosted by the *Gazette*. She was often mocked by staff for saying "telephone" instead of "phone," enunciating the word too clearly every time. *When I heard he was running for Vice Mayor I said to Susan, 'Susan, get him on the TELE-PHONE immediately.'*

At the party, he remembered glimpsing her for only a few moments. Her green flowing dress and sleek, set hair made her look like a plant, like one of the many types of foliage surrounding the room, blending her into her environment. Her jungly look in combination with the live plants cast a feral filter over the entire room as well as the rest of the guests. Graham had stood up against a load-bearing beam the whole time, taking full advantage of its ability to bear loads. Others at the party could only see about half of his face at one time given his angle against the beam. He didn't like parties, especially work parties.

"They said Dad was calling himself Erie Moseby. He insisted that was his name. The thing is, he doesn't remember running away, creating a new identity, anything. The doctor said he's in recovery, which means he remembers his real life, his life with us, but doesn't remember running away. Oh, it's awful. When can you visit him?" Delia said.

"Where is he?" Graham asked.

"Some facility. I don't know if it's a hospital or a nursing home or what. They all sort of look the same."

*

His sister had been right. The facility is unclear and unmarked so that residents would not be labeled. But all buildings are starting to look the same to Graham. He thinks it would be easy to slip into another life, to slip into something strikingly different and not really know it had happened. He is surprised that not everyone experiences this condition of his father's at least once. He wonders where his father got his fugue name, Erie Moseby.

*

Graham and his sister talk more often now, mostly about their father and his current state. They say he has completely recovered from the fugue but now has dementia.

Talking to Delia reminds him of when they grew up together. When he was young and always too small for his grade, carrying books thicker than his arms.

Their mother would do the wash but not want to dry her more delicate items in the dryer, so on certain days for hours there would be bras and underwear strung up on hooks, posts, doorknobs, whatever was available around the house. It made him think of a butcher with slabs of meat hung everywhere, swaying and cold as death. She would also sing or hum all the time, but only one line of a song, over and over through the hall. Never more than one line. These were not songs other people sang or even recognized. Graham wasn't sure if his mother made them up or if they were just so old no one else remembered them anymore.

He also thought of secrets. Delia and their mother always told obscene amounts of secrets to each other, back and forth. Graham was never involved. Delia knew when her mother was leaving. She actually told her own daughter ahead of time as if they were co-conspirators. He never knew what to make of this. Delia told him what was happening right after she had left. He was finishing up a math worksheet at the time. He got distracted and had erased a wrong answer too vigorously, forcing the metal on the pencil to scratch the cheap worksheet paper until it tore, bunching it up like an accordion.

*

Graham's car has a flat tire so he is taking the bus to see his father. Beside him, a woman speaks over the phone fluidly in Spanish. She switches to English a few minutes in as the bus groans into a curve, then seamlessly back to Spanish, articulate and equally confident in both. It is effortless for her, Graham notices. Graham's phone isn't getting a good connection on this bus. He can't even check his email.

He studies her. It is like looking at himself; he has no idea what he looks like, really. Every picture of himself is like a new person, similar but morphed somehow. Staring into a mirror doesn't help. He likes to think of himself as incredibly dynamic and to make everyone else caricatures. Reduced. As if he has some level of depth others do not possess. His co-worker is always angry; his neighbor is consistently beautiful. But he, he changes into a wolf at certain hours of the day. This woman, he thinks he is able to see the complexity in her like he can see it in himself. This makes him appreciative, feeling connected to her in some way. Everyone else on the bus, all of their faces are vague in an almost violent way.

He reluctantly leaves the woman, gets off the bus to visit with his father. The snow around the sidewalk is firmly packed. It is strong and unwavering but of course he knows it will melt eventually.

Of Course

The grass was the sturdy kind, the wide, waxy blades with the little pinstripes. There's something solidifying about that, she thought.

*

"Did you get a good deal?" asked her mother on the phone.

"Yes," she wavered.

"Well, what was it?"

"I'm not sure."

"You're not sure?"

"No."

"Well how do you know it's good?"

"Frank handles all of that stuff. He said it was a good price. Very reasonable."

*

There was a man standing outside in those thick blades taking out the sign and suddenly everything felt very flimsy under her. There was a loose tile. A tree creaked and occasionally groaned, hovering over one of the back windows. But Penelope started to cry and then she knew she would never get them fixed.

All the rooms were covered with cardboard. Every time she smelled cardboard, she thought she smelled pizza, because it reminded her of pizza boxes, and she would have to order pizza for dinner.

*

When she finally rid herself of boxes, she was able to go to the store and stock up on vegetables. The cashier handed her the receipt and said, "Have a good day," to her while staring at the opposite wall.

*

"Mother, you know the difference between older women and younger women?"

"I can think of several."

"When older women walk into a restroom together, their conversation ends when they close the stalls."

"And the younger women?"

"Well, they keep going."

Her mother paused to inhale a cigarette or take a sip of something, or maybe just to gather herself.

"How are the women there?" her mother finally asked.

"They go out for coffee and one says 'of course' and the other says 'of course' back and I'm not so sure what they mean."

"Hmm."

"Plus I think I'm the only one who wants to be with her husband."

"Well yes, that will happen."

*

A car with a booming bass drove by and shook the whole face of the house. Even the floorboards rattled a bit. She pretended not to notice and instead tried to recall a special she had seen on TV about mummies holing up all their riches in their tombs.

*

A neighbor came by with a lasagna which she thought was very caring albeit old-fashioned. This woman, Gracie, had stolen her way inside and inspected the front room.

"I just finished decorating and feel a bit more settled," she explained to her new neighbor.

"Well, you certainly have a style," said Gracie.

"Thank you," she said, though she realized as she said it that maybe that wasn't a compliment.

"What do you do?" asked Gracie.

"I'm a nurse, though I've cut down to about two days a week because of my daughter."

"That's very sensible. Very well-balanced."

She did not thank Gracie this time. She waited.

"Of course I never really did buy into the whole traditional medicine thing. I think vitamins can cure just about anything," explained Gracie.

She felt the lasagna grow very hot against her fingertips.

"Well, I should put this away. Thanks again."

*

Gracie left and she snapped Penelope in her car seat and drove north on the interstate. She put the windows down all the way but could not get enough air in the car. She wasn't convinced she was breathing. She accelerated faster than she thought she ever would with Penelope in the car, then slowed way down. Eventually, she turned around and drove back.

*

Once after dinner, she heard shrill yelping coming from next door but it sounded like it was occurring in the same room. The children outside were either being terrorized or experiencing playful freedom. They both sort of sound the same, she thought, and assumed it was the latter.

*

"Do chimney sweeps still exist?" she asked her mother.

This particular afternoon was very long.

"Yes, I think they do."

This was somehow comforting to her.

*

Sometimes at night she would wake up and everything would look very strange in the dark. She wouldn't know where she was or who was next to her or what she was doing. Eventually, she would fall back asleep.

*

She was changing when she noticed a woman wandering in her backyard. She finished getting dressed but did not take her eyes off the woman who was now pacing near a row of sunflowers. She opened the back door.

"Have you seen a dog? A big fluffy one?" the woman asked before she could say anything.

"No, I haven't."

"I'm sorry, I'm in your yard and I'm sweating and I'm feeling pretty dumb," the woman admitted.

"It's okay." She felt a strange urge to put her at ease.

"I must look pretty helpless, huh?" the woman asked.

Her words were carefully formed as they left her mouth, a savoring of syllables, a signpost of intentionality.

"Ah hell. I don't think I really care about finding this dog anyway. He would look at me and his eyes would be filled with such disdain." The woman moved closer to her.

She shrugged, not knowing the dog.

"I'm Avery. There's a flea market today. Do you want to go with me?"

"Sure. Let me get my kid."

*

The three of them trudged through the alleys and fumbled with trinkets as they went. Penelope enjoyed chewing on discarded price tags.

"At first, I felt ashamed that I was apathetic about my job, but then I realized it was perfect because it gave me something to complain about. To blame all my shortcomings on, you know?" the woman said.

She nodded.

"Do you and your husband want to come over for dinner?" asked Avery.

"Yes."

*

This time, her mother had called her.

"Are you coming home for Thanksgiving at least?"

"I'm pretty sure but I've still got to talk it over with Frank."

She looked around the room. She knew this was her home. She knew it was her home because it was 4:00pm and she knew exactly how the sun was going to hit the furniture and which objects would be lit up from the window.

"Well, just let me know once you find out."

"Okay. Listen, I've got to go."

Back Row

Professor Wynn,

I'm sure you're aware of the rumors about you. I'm sure I'm not the only student writing you a letter about it. Though I must ask, because I'm rather out of practice, why do you require a letter? Isn't that a little old-fashioned? I heard it was because you love writing letters. That you write them so habitually and fluidly that you're athletic about your letter-writing. I also heard it's because you're lonely. I just started writing this letter and I'm already insulting you, so clearly I'm off to a good start.

I hesitated writing you because I couldn't possibly believe this would do anything for me. But yesterday, using the bathroom at the end of the hall on the 2nd floor of the Arts & Sciences building, none of the automatic faucets or paper towel dispensers would recognize my frantic waving and I thought maybe I could be a ghost. This would not have been my only clue. And then, as if mocking me, I saw a scrap of paper towel on the floor. It was shaped like a leaf as if it were attempting to reincarnate.

So I thought I'd give this a shot. And though I love this city filled with people who are a little too blunt and probably wear sweatshirts too often, and I even love the winters with their melancholic wisps of snow, but the winters here are too long. It is now, as you know, sufficiently warm outside, but I feel like I'm still fighting the chill of a few months ago.

You were seen sitting with two students (young, rather cute girls) I don't really know, just social-media-know, outside on a bench in front of the student center, so I'm assuming I'm too late for this, but I have to try.

Below are the reasons why, if those aforementioned rumors are true, I deserve to visit Thailand:

1. I've never been out of the country. Canada doesn't really count. My roommate studied abroad in Italy last semester and she came back saying things like, "You know how Italian men are always picking you up," and I don't. Or "You know what those little noodles are called that look like ears," and I don't.

2. Because I'm tired of listening to the susurrus of the leaky water heater in the hall closet that sounds like the roar of a crowd when I wake up in the night, as if many people are cheering me on to pee. (Here I go talking about using the restroom in this letter TWICE now.) I'd rather hear the gulf outside your townhouse on the outskirts of Bangkok. My roommate and I often discuss who will call the landlord about the water heater but it's

the whole "diffusion of responsibility" principle at work. Like the Kitty Genovese case without the murder. Or at least I think, I *assume*, no lives have ended over something like this.

3. I bought all of these tiny, bright plants in equally tiny, bright containers to display in every room of my apartment. I dutifully watered them but they died off anyway, one by one. Such melodramatic plants. I dumped the dead plants, cleaned their containers and left them out dazzlingly empty.

4. When I was twelve, we visited my aunt in Boston and we all thought it'd be fun to go on a whale watch downtown. We saw no whales. Not even a lump of trash in the harbor that could be mistaken for a tail.

5. Because I have two states: I'm either trying to humor my father or deliberately trying not to humor him.

6. I saw this girl at dinner the other night who looked really familiar. I couldn't place her at first, but after staring for too long, I figured it out. The girl was one of my selves. I have always imagined myself as three potential people, three possible outcomes living in three very distinct ways. This girl was the slightly chubby, overly confident self I had not become. I thought that self might try for something like this.

7. Everyone has a tell, like in poker. Every time I start recounting a story this guy who is supposed to be my best friend immediately gulps at his water bottle. That's

his tell. He gulps the water as if desperately wanting to sustain himself, help fight against the asinine.

8. Because I can say "Bangkok" without laughing. And that's more than I can say about that best friend of mine.

9. Learning French in middle school, I would always get my pronouns confused. "I" is "Je," not "tu" or "vous," I remember now. You are not me. I am not you. But why not? Professor Wynn, why not get as close as we can?

10. Maybe it's my extreme affinity for order, but I thought it was appropriate to list ten reasons. When looking through missed calls or unread texts or even emails that I don't want to respond to, I ease my guilt by saying, "I could be busy. I could be very busy." And I've been saying that a lot.

I just noticed that I am pressing my pen hard into this paper and my words are making a substantial impact. There are indents like braille on the pages. I think it's because I want them to make a substantial impact on you. I will probably type this up before I send it to you, but forgive my exuberance. It can be as gruesome as a tuber freshly plucked from underground. (I used to live on a potato farm.) But I don't want to be underground any longer. If you really do let students stay at your townhouse, please consider me.

Sincerely,

Back Row, Fourth Seat from Your Left

Pirates

Hitchhiking, it turned out, was not like the movies. The last time she walked down this sidewalk had been when she was dutifully attending dance class, hair slicked into a tight bun, pink tights thick with a few snags, sucking in her black leotard at the middle. She would try to crunch as many leaves under her feet as she went because she liked the sound.

Today she could not play the leaf game. She left the day of the horrific storm that blew through after only a few minutes. The leaves were still wet. Right before it began, the high winds arrived and she watched a man fight hard against it, the wind blowing against his t-shirt so that it accentuated his rotund belly. A gaping hole for his bellybutton impressed in the shirt and was shaped like a mouth in shock.

Ballet classes were a long time ago. She was years out of school and other extracurricular activities but people treated her as if that wasn't the case, so she went along with it. She blamed it on her small frame to comfort herself.

She is a woman with very dark hair cut in a harsh, almost boyish shape. She is small, so small that she could be mistaken for a young girl easily if she didn't have that exuberant cut in combination with a keen, deliberate sense of what to wear that only adults seemed to have. Like her black scoop neck dress with the mildly low back.

It didn't feel that long ago anyway, growing up and being in school. School, where teachers told students they could be anything they wanted to be and didn't tell them how.

She had reached the T-intersection with the small plaza where her father liked to go for dry cleaning because it was cheap. A gray Toyota Camry with rust along the bottom rolled up to the stop sign while the window was rolled down. The driver had noticed her signature thumb thrown out at the last second, almost forgotten.

She got in wordlessly, already looking out of the windshield to the stretch of road ahead. He smelled of an emergency brake left on for too long, the acrid burn of forgetfulness. He was what her friends would call "okay," a guy who could fade into a crowd rather easily.

In the silence she thought about her first time on an airplane. Her body alerting her that she was no longer on the ground where she lived, where she needed to be for survival. The disorientation and the dissociation of it. Wanting to scream but becoming more silent. The rows of people seated and too calm for what was happening. Being somewhere at some time and then suddenly being somewhere completely different. Not like the road where you can presumably feel every mile. Where the change can sink in.

After they reached the bordering borough, he asked almost uselessly, "Where do you want to go?"

"Away," she said.

"Name's Chris."

"Victoria," she said, trying it out for the first time.

She noticed that the back seat was empty except for a very worn looking dictionary with curled edges and a few broken guitar picks.

Chris, it turned out, played shows at a local bar & grill in exchange for a free dinner every night. Besides a small disability check, he had no other means and was trying to expand his reach to other bars for actual monetary payment.

Maybe they could instead travel all the way across the country to the other coast. Maybe they could rent a nice place with a very white pool with very blue water. Her thoughts became loftier as the car slowly climbed up the mountain.

Chris made little whale sounds when he thought of something pleasant.

They stopped at a gas station/convenience store/grimy diner. Her legs stuck a few times sliding into the red booth.

"No one's taking it away from you," he said as she ate her cheeseburger.

She stood outside to stretch before getting back in the car. A flock of crows flew overhead. "Did you know a bunch of crows is called a murder?" he said, suddenly behind her. The air was thick with humidity, humid with possibility.

They returned to the car and steadily traveled along the road again. She thought they had made it pretty far until she saw the farmer's market her father used to take her to every fall. She would sprint through the corn maze, beg for a jar of apple butter, get dangerously close to the goats in their pens. Her brother would think the painted scenes with cutouts to place your head were much more hilarious than they actually were. He would place his head in the hole and be someone else entirely: a woman with a polka dot bikini top and daisy dukes.

"What exactly are you trying to get away from?" he asked.

She made up a dramatic story peppered with abuse. She realized that if he asked her about it again later she would probably not remember.

*

They stood around a wall the color of terracotta and it made their skin look more flushed and youthful than it actually was. Chris introduced her to his friends as Victoria, saying her name loudly as if patting himself on the back for remembering it.

She did a full, slow turn around the room, uninterested in the conversation. A woman with asymmetrical hair spoke to a man in a gravelly voice. Her hair was a vibrant contrast; one side almost shaved and the other side waving, flowing, seemingly endlessly down her back. In one corner, a plain looking girl struggled to talk with an articulate woman who knew how to accessorize. She gulped some bourbon from her cup and Chris found his way to her.

"Are you even old enough to be drinking?" he said, grinning.

She shrugged as if she didn't know, took another sip. She turned to her side to overhear another conversation. "They say you shouldn't smoke if you're pregnant. I'm not much of a smoker myself, but I think the only time a cigarette would really sound good is if I found out I was pregnant," a woman shouted to her friend.

She drifted over to a couch set up directly across from a sizeable TV that was turned off. Chris found her again and sat beside her. She knew how nice those TVs were, how clear the picture was.

Chris stared into a burning candle and asked, "Did you know something that is viscous has a low viscosity?"

She shook her head.

"You must be tired," he said.

He led her to a vacant bedroom that was surprisingly clean. She looked mildly concerned and he patted her on the head, shut the door behind him, wandering back into the party. The bed was comfortable and forgiving. She didn't know how it could be comfortable and forgiving.

*

When Chris showed her his place, she asked, "Where's the dog? I expected you to have a dog," and she immediately went exploring.

She found that Chris refused to finish lotions, deodorants, everything, not wanting to use the last bits of anything. She wondered if it was because he was lazy or if it reminded him of his mortality to use the last of something. Containers flooded his drawers.

She looked at all the empty containers and she thought about Gertrude Stein. How she fastidiously trimmed her hedges while France was being occupied by Germany. How people obsess over the seemingly mundane to distract themselves from the tragic. How her life was far from tragic, rather calm and relatively kind, but that life was enough tragedy on its own.

She followed Chris to his gigs and jumped back in his rusted car each time, driving up and down the mountain with him, over and back. Chris lived near a go-kart track and when you were stopped at the traffic light you could hear the announcer frantically trying to pull children out of the go-karts with just the power of his words.

When she was tired of the gigs and they went on too late into the night, too early in the morning, she would get irritable. She would snap at him on the way back to his house, then pat his leg affectionately to make up for the harshness in her voice.

*

She walked to the store to grab a few things and ran into the Cruzes, old family friends. She saw them coming in their overly textured sweaters, blinking expectantly. They were getting old. Mr. Cruze grunted and spewed like an old man now, difficult to listen to without thinking of the death behind it. Mrs. Cruze asked how her father and brother were. She said they were just fine but she didn't know if they were just fine or not.

Mrs. Cruze chirped like she was over-caffeinated. She talked about how good it was to see her and how nice she looked.

"You are so *encouraging*," she replied to Mrs. Cruze, but it didn't come out sounding very complimentary.

Walking back from the store, she thought about what she was trying not to think about. It wasn't that her father and brother were powerless like they imagined themselves to be, rather that they were too powerful. She cared too much what they thought and said. She required approving glances from them every time she passed in front of their eyes.

She thought of the Cruzes' daughter, Virginia, who used to come over and play in the basement with her. They found a box full of cleaned and buffed seashells, insects pinned delicately to matted paper and trapped behind glass, browned tortoise shells chipped away at the edges. They called themselves pirates and used the tortoise shells as currency, already understanding innately the necessity of bartering.

*

That evening, she and Chris rode back from a late show reeking of stale smoke. They were waiting by the light at the go-kart track once again. The recording of the announcer had accidentally been left on though the track had been closed for several hours.

"Your ride has come to an end. Please pull into the pit area and remain seated."

"Did you know that a retinue is a group of trusted advisors or assistants?" asked Chris.

"Your ride has come to —"

"I like the sound of that word. Retinue. Ret-in-ue," he continued.

"— pit area and remain seated."

She nodded and kept her eye on the light.

"Your ride has come to an end. Please pull into the pit area and remain –"

The light turned green. Chris went to bed as soon as they entered the house but she wasn't ready for sleep just yet. She stayed up to assemble some new furniture. She stared at the instructions for assembly, the gold glow of the overhead light touching the page. She read and waited until she understood the instructions. She wanted more instructions.

Talisman

I followed someone. This person, Claudia, I knew her a long time ago. I had never followed anyone before but now it's hard for me to imagine that I haven't been doing it for a very long time. I'm somewhat of a natural. This is very strange because I'm not a natural at anything.

I had a job. Somehow I had been weaned off practically all the responsibilities of this job without my noticing. I have since noticed. This was much worse than losing a job. They seemed to keep me around to fulfill a deeply entrenched nuclear family dynamic they all shared and required on a relational level. And that's all they needed me for. I loathed my lack of utility, and this loathing gave me enough energy to get me up each day for work. When I wasn't in a state of loathing, I was in a state of bewilderment that loathing could have the power to keep me in this negative cycle, and the bewilderment tucked me in at night.

I felt about as necessary as the first "r" in February. It reminded me of lying in bed as a child on those longest of summer days when it was still light out at bedtime. I would lie there staring at the crack of light where the blinds met the window, hearing the neighborhood kids (with more laissez-faire parents) shriek in freedom.

It's easy to say I should have known from the beginning. I interviewed alongside a guy applying for a different position and my future supervisor gave us a tour of the building together. Each time I had a question or comment, my supervisor wouldn't acknowledge me. He would look at the guy next to me and answer as if he asked the question, or he would keep moving. For several months after being hired, if I had an idea in a meeting, he adjusted his glasses while I spoke, as if what I was saying was too incredulous to be real.

But my desk was near a window and that was nice. I could see planes ascending astonishingly close to this window each morning, but I never saw them coming back in and I took this as a good sign. My other coworkers were tolerable and some were even fun to be around. They were paying me money to be there, too.

*

I ran into Claudia on the street returning home from work. I heard an ice cream truck and felt so nostalgic about it that I walked down a parallel street to snag a quick look. Who knows how many days we had been traveling so close to each other unknowingly. Who knows if she ever went down that street except this one time.

My first reaction upon seeing her was a slow recognition of who she was. This recognition then morphed into an urgency to avoid her. Because what was I going to do, catch up with her? Make small talk?

She was wearing a very colorful, very floral dress that was a little too summery for the beginning of March, with a light sweater overtop. The sweater had a pretty noticeable hole in the sleeve and looked so fragile and papery that I was expecting the whole thing to unravel onto the sidewalk. I darted away but she caught me.

Even with the holey sweater she had the stately, regal manner she's always had. Claudia seems like the kind of person who would actually use a hotel safe when she travels. I was wearing something semi-professional but felt suddenly mangy.

We were in the same second grade class and grew up in such a remote area that we were in the same class for all the following grades as well. We were never really friends.

I remember she pronounced "realtor" as if there were an "i" in the middle of it and she laughed like a Valley Girl on the wrong coast and she was our valedictorian. I heard she ended up as a civil engineer and then I also heard she was an assistant manager at a Yankee Candle Company in the mall.

We made some trite greetings and she told me she was going to meet George and Grace and John Carlisle for dinner with this look of intense meaning that I couldn't decipher because I didn't know who these people were. This dinner was either especially exciting or grotesque from what I could make of her expression.

"Gwen, George actually suggested we meet at Bailey's, can you believe it?"

I could believe it, but that's because I still didn't know what she was talking about. It's like she thought we had lived the same life and knew all the same people but I had somehow forgotten all the great stories contained in this life. She was so confident in her context and expectation of understanding that I felt I needed to apologize to her, or at least to go along with it. So I nodded a lot.

I made a polite comment about needing to take my dog out for a walk. I gave her a cordial arm squeeze as a goodbye and she ran off to dinner. A note fell out of her pocket and I happened to accidentally notice it fluttering to the ground. Suffused with enough curiosity to pick it up, I actually had to pounce on it before the wind got to it.

*

It said:
Max 8pm Thursday
Azaleas or hydrangeas
Dr. Fineberg – make appt

Then something indecipherable below that bled into a coffee stain. I didn't know anyone still wrote paper notes to themselves.

*

I didn't necessarily want to see her but I found myself trying to find her anyway. What if she really needed this note? What if Dr. Fineberg was performing surgery on an organ of hers obscenely littered with tumors?

I was going to the grocery store and then I was going past the grocery store. I was late for a gallery opening and then I was pushing onward in the opposite direction of the gallery.

After doing some research earlier that week, I had enough of an idea of where to look for her. I ended up being right but having to wait in a parking garage for over an hour. The concrete floor beneath my feet had blended seamlessly with old gum and stains of unknown provenance.

Amazed at my own ability to wait, I saw that Claudia had appeared, making her way to her car. She had that same sweater on with a different dress. I remembered that it would be unusual for me to be there, note in hand, so I panicked and jumped in my car, tailing her instead.

I didn't watch cop movies but I knew that you were supposed to let at least one car in between you and the person you were tailing, so after a couple of minutes, I finagled this by letting in a morose PT Cruiser.

*

In fourth grade, I copied her every movement. She tucked her hair behind her ear, I tucked my hair behind my ear. She doodled a picture of a frog on her word search worksheet, I drew a (better looking) frog on mine.

She was always overly enthusiastic about mundane events. *That spill looks exactly like a stegosaurus! I really need a Golden Delicious apple right now and if I had one it would be the most perfect snack.*

I distinctly remember overhearing her tell a friend in the hallway by her locker, "There is nothing more fatal than purchasing sensible shoes." It was sophomore year. It was the same year I tried running track.

There were rumors about Claudia and the history teacher/renowned soccer coach that I never believed then but was maybe starting to believe now.

*

The morning I put in my two weeks' notice, the water beaded on the shower wall in such perfectly spaced lines that it looked like a record that couldn't make its way back around.

I wanted to disrupt the office dynamics by finally leaving. I couldn't understand why people would want more family when I loved mine and was still terrible to them. I get so nervous about being the irresponsible one that I send birthday cards especially early to ease my mind. But then I worry that I send them too early; that it would seem like I didn't know when my family's birthdays actually are, which is somehow much worse.

*

I managed to fumble into the grocery store where Claudia had parked. I made grabbing some strawberry-banana yogurt look like a serendipitous occasion. I couldn't find a way to bring up the note and ended up accepting an invitation to a girls' weekend at Claudia's aunt's cabin instead.

I discovered that girls' cabin weekends entail day-drinking and binge-watching shows and ignoring the surrounding nature altogether. We were in a pleasant paralysis. The weekend was disorienting and strange.

*

Claudia carries three separate cell phones at all times. She is a family plan unto herself. The phones are for work purposes but she can't really explain why. She leaves detailed messages for everyone she knows, talking to the voicemail as if the person answered. And when I get these voicemails now, sometimes I actually understand the context.

How to Become Unemployed (in 10 Easy Steps)

1. First, you should graduate from college with a major like Western European Architecture, or Postcolonial Literature, or Interdisciplinary Liberal Studies in Humanity. Be very passionate about your major. Be overcome with solving the world's problems in a sort of hypomanic state. Mistake self-absorption with concrete ideals. Find it difficult to quit volunteering for fundraisers and playing ultimate frisbee. Apply for research positions at local non-profit organizations. You want to remain here; you like the feel of a university town.

2. Start working for one of those non-profits. Buy "work clothes" from JCPenney. Begin thinking your job defines you as a person. Browse briefcases and laptop bags online when you come home from work. Get the feeling you are helping people.

3. After about three months, realize that at work you don't really see people at all, let alone help them with anything. Feel isolated. Disappear into a large system. Get nauseated from the taupe walls and the gray carpet

and the subtle flicker of the screen at your desk. Become disillusioned. Feel sneaky when you wear jeans for a week straight and no one notices. Then realize that no one really even looks at you when you speak to them. As you attempt to write grant proposals, question how to spell very simple words. Stare at them. Think they look funny. Think that can't possibly be how you spell "home".

4. Apply to grad school. Sleep in the morning of the GRE. Roll over, fluff your pillow and mutter antonyms to your subconscious.

5. Start dating a poet. Embrace the second-hand smoke. Imagine your lungs speckling and blackening. Take a strange comfort from that image.

6. Think other people are much happier than you.

7. At work, start rushing through your daily tasks. Time yourself. Finish everything by lunch and ride the elevator up and down for the rest of the day. Ask people strange questions in the elevator and occasionally throw in horribly cheesy jokes. Ask, "If this is an elevator, where is the elevator music?" and "Why is there carpet on the walls? Should there be windows on the floor?" Contemplate the numerous, reproducing germs swarming all over the buttons. Make trite, meaningless analogies about the ups and downs of life as the elevator rises and falls.

8. Follow this work-til-lunch-then-elevator procedure for the next month. Become a truly silly person. Make

people whisper about you in the corner of the elevator.

9. Fall into a mild depression. Dump the poet. Stop waking up in the morning. Have only one thing on your to-do list: apply for disability. See a counselor from the Employee Assistance Program. Check boxes for helplessness, hopelessness, worthlessness, uselessness – anything that ends in "ness." Know on a completely different level what it's like to receive a quizzical look.

10. Buy lots of new inventions and cosmetics from QVC. Start sending some of the QVC packages to your grandmother. Start sending them to strangers' addresses. Start making up addresses to send them to and see if they don't get sent back. Lift up the blinds and stare out until your eyeballs feel scorched. Close your eyes and make a story out of the blotchy remainders.

RE: West Property

From: Clark Hartman

To: Darcie West

RE: West Property

August 18, 2015 at 10:15am

Automatic Reply:

I will be out of the office starting Tuesday, August 18th to Thursday, August 20th with limited access to email. If this is an urgent matter, please contact Cindy at the front desk at stewart.cindy@hlassociates.com.

Thank you,

Clark Hartman

Confidentiality Notice: Content in this message may not be forwarded without the express written consent of Clark Hartman. This email is confidential and may be protected by attorney-client privileges. If you have received this message in error, please notify the sender by replying and then deleting message.

On Tue August 18, 2015 at 10:14am, Delia West
<deliareneewest57@gmail.com> wrote:

Clark,

I've attached the scanned and signed copy of the form. I'll be eager to hear what they find, as I've already found some surprising items on the property myself.

Out back, I watched a bunny giving birth in a pile of old grass clippings and yard waste. She looked completely shocked, as if she had no idea what was happening. Maybe she didn't. Maybe she has no idea how procreating works. Do you think other bunnies have explained it to her? Or do all species inherently know about that stuff? I'll have to look it up. I'm sure it's baffling enough to give birth, let alone not knowing that all these beings are going to come out of you. I felt bad for her. I wanted to help her but I didn't know how.

I'm sorry if this is too much. I'm infested with sensibilities. Growing up I made sure to include every stuffed animal during my make-believe time so as to not hurt any of their feelings. And even now I take the price tags off my bargain used books because I feel they should not be subjected to their supposed monetary value, especially not right there on the front cover.

Anyway, besides the bunny, I found a completely intact set of stairs (?!) in the thickness of the backwoods (within property lines). As you might already know, my Grandpa didn't have another house back there, not even the skeleton of a shack nearby, in order to explain it. I think this might be a good omen. If you know anyone who needs extra stairs, tell them to email me.

Thirdly, there was a large receptacle found on the edge of the property by the highway. It looks like it rolled off a semi and was intended to eventually belong on a train. I haven't even tried to figure out how to open it yet. I have enough freight, so to speak, to deal with already. Or maybe it's more like my mind is a cement truck constantly spinning and making me dizzy with sludge. That's probably a better analogy.

Am I "on the clock" with you while you read these emails? Please let me know.

I'm sorry if I'm all over the place. I obviously loved Grandpa and I'm also a bit rankled right now because a complete stranger walked by me in the office parking lot and touched my face without saying anything. His palm firmly cupped my cheek. I know that's really nothing but it sort of disrupted my whole day. He just walked away after that. He had those teardrops tattooed on his face so he definitely murdered several people. Other than that, he seemed like a rather polite individual. I'm just trying not to think about it.

Let me know if you need anything else and please keep me updated on what they find!

Thanks,

Darcie

On Fri August 14, 2015 at 3:33pm, Clark Hartman
<hartman.clark@hlassociates.com> wrote:

Ms. West,

Please complete the form within the next week to ensure expedient leasing procedures. It is with your benefit in mind that I write this.

Regards,

Clark Hartman

Confidentiality Notice: Content in this message may not be forwarded without the express written consent of Clark Hartman. This email is confidential and may be protected by attorney-client privileges. If you have received this message in error, please notify the sender by replying and then deleting message.

On Mon July 27, 2015 at 11:53am, Delia West
<deliareneewest57@gmail.com> wrote:

Mr. Hartman,

I still can't get over all this. It was good to meet with you, but since then I've started repeating myself a lot. I was worried at first about early onset dementia, but then I accepted that it's just my mind's way of taking in reality, a way to let the facts sink in that couldn't possibly be true (but are actually true).

I'm a bit frantic as the scorched breakroom coffee burns a deep pit into my stomach and sends little shoots of adrenaline down the line of veins in my forearms, but has also somehow sedated me, numbed my brain even.

To organize my thoughts, here are some things I remember about my Grandpa, or Cole West, as you call him:

1. He was very sick for such a long time, but not quite sick enough to die, that I just got used to him that way. I forgot that things could get better or worse for him. I'm sort of rueful about not asking him more questions about himself and Grandma Joan now that I can't anymore, which I guess is pretty typical.

2. He had this melancholy jockey statue holding up a lantern in his front bed by the hydrangeas, and the lantern always creaked when it swayed in the violent gusts during the spring. The wind can get so strong up there that it becomes more ominous than the worst thunderstorms, since it leaves no marks of its presence or warning of its starting up again. The air the wind brings in always has a yeasty, sweet, almost taunting smell to it from the distillery.

3. He was missing the tip of his right pointer finger. There was just a scabby stub at the end of it. He would point at things for me to get him while he was sitting

in his Barcalounger and I would just stare at the stump, completely frozen. I would also stare at Grandma Joan's smile. She had an excess of gums that made her teeth look like little white pebbles in comparison, like the afterthought of a riverbed.

4. They lived across from the Pattisons. Are the Pattisons still living there? I went to school with Jake Pattison. I think they moved but I'll always remember Jake because in 2nd grade he had many "accidents". Then in 3rd grade, we were in the same class again with this girl who at 8 years old had (excuse me) already fully developed and she had a thin but complete mustache above her lip like a furry isosceles of hormones. This girl beat up poor Jake on the playground swiftly and without remorse. It was tantalizing to watch the blood flow from the cracks of his chapped lips. He was always licking his lips so it's no wonder they were chapped all the time. He picked mulch and shredded tire from his hair with great shame. I wonder how he's doing.

I'm so distracted. My desk is right beside the bathrooms and I hear the constant whirring of the automatic paper towel dispenser. Plus, the automatic soap refuses to acknowledge my existence when I'm in there. Why does everything have to be automatic these days?

Last time I was in there a woman was vigorously rubbing at a stain on the crotch of her pants, blocking the only paper towel dispenser. I know it's a restroom but have a little decorum, you know?

Thanks again for meeting with me. I'll get that paperwork filled out right away.

Sincerely,

Darcie

On Mon July 27, 2015 at 9:47am, Clark Hartman <hartman.clark@hlassociates.com> wrote:

Ms. West,

Thank you for meeting with me regarding the recently inherited property of your grandfather, Mr. Cole West.

Please complete the Natural Gas Lease form attached and send a signed copy back if you have decided to go through with the request for natural gas exploration on the property. I will contact you regarding the damage to the driveway from unauthorized vehicles shortly. Since your grandfather put up a sign discouraging motorists from using his driveway as a turnaround at the dead end of the street, there may be something we can do.

Let me know if you have any questions or concerns.

Regards,

Clark Hartman

Where Things Should Go

She was sitting at the end of her couch when she realized what would lead to her death. Her carelessness. It would be some accident. Something avoidable and humiliating, the opposite of noble. Like when someone asked her how she had broken her arm in the fifth grade and she had to say she tripped over the dishwasher door until it dawned on her that she could lie.

It was so obvious now, the way she would ultimately end things. Macie ran into walls on a regular basis. Just clipped her shoulder, really, nothing bad. But these incidents would probably build into something larger once she was elderly, she decided. Her certainty was oceanic, listing in her mind like violent waves. She fell asleep on the couch with these thoughts and a pen in her hand. The blue ink stain blossomed on the ivory pillow until it resembled a fresh bruise.

Macie stayed in, mostly, and observed her roommate. She lived with a girlish woman named Jill with a lineless face and hair that smelled like perfume even after a humid run through the neighborhood. Jill had a decorator's eye and had made their bungalow look much more impressive than it actually was. Jill frowned when she discovered the pillow.

When watching Jill with her endless string of energy became too tiring, Macie would meet Yale and Raine and Sven at the only pizza place in town. She dwelled on the fact that she surrounded herself with people who had names like ancient monosyllabic warriors.

*

The fields on the left side of the main road heading west were flat with expertly wrapped bales of hay. The fields on the right were Amish fields; flat with occasional large piles of hay instead of rolls, and dotted with black and white clothes hung on a line. There would always be one tree amid the flatness on each farm near the edge like a relief, with spindly branches and a thick trunk, a full and rounded canopy.

She passed the fields going to Yale's house. His blue house on Blue Avenue. Yale was her closest friend of what she called the Leftover Friends. They were Macie's brother's friends first and she had glommed onto them while he packed up and flew away for long term medical missions.

It turned out that Yale was a great friend, even a best friend, though she avoided the term. The others, Sven and Raine, she tolerated, tried not to dwell on their faults.

Yale was one of those guys with such dark, full eyelashes that it looked like he constantly applied eyeliner to his lower lids. Macie thought he would have made a good vampire. He was a bit chunky but with a taut, angular face that did not reveal his excess mass. He could take a rather flattering headshot or driver's license picture, but Macie had not seen any of these types of photos anywhere, had not consciously looked for them at least.

Raine lived with Yale in the blue house on Blue Avenue. Raine had a terrible affinity for stealing other people's mail. He had piles and piles scattered all over the house of greeting cards, credit card offers, notes from grandmothers scrawled in florid cursive and thick, glossy magazines catering to middle aged women.

Together, they liked to restore the old blue house built in 1905. Raine had told Macie about the real plaster walls, how back then they used patches of horse hair mingled in the plaster for strength. The floors were original too and had shrunk so that there were large gaps between the pine boards.

*

Macie looked at her phone to discover that Yale had left her a message 45 minutes earlier. *Come over stat! Bring some wine!* She didn't reply, just threw on her jacket and got in her car.

Had he eloped with a stranger? Did he get an atrocious tattoo? Had Raine finally killed someone? The options were endless. Her exuberance for imagining devastating fates for her closest friends only mildly concerned her as she passed the expansive fields.

She imagined the murderous Raine being arrested, going down to the station for fingerprints, and remembered the only time she had that experience. It was in school; she assumed now it was in case of child abduction. The whole class did it and when she lined up and put her finger on the inkpad, then onto the paper, she thought the mark was giving her some sort of an identity, rather impressing her own identity on the paper.

Yale was alone but seemed excited, not concerned for his roommate's imaginary arrest or his own difficulties.

"Guess what?" he said.

"I can't possibly."

"Alright, I'll just tell you. I won the lottery!"

"What?"

"Yeah, weird, right? I had never bought a ticket before and went down to the 4-Way Market sort of as a joke. Raine had to tell me that I won because I forgot to check. Still in disbelief. How crazy is this?"

She had no response. She imagined the patches of horse hair in the walls bristling. A horse forming, roaring to life, breaking through.

He didn't wait for her response. "Did you bring the wine? I thought we could celebrate."

She touched the sides of her legs as if checking pockets. "I apologize, it seems as if I'm only cleverly disguised as an adult. I had no wine in the house."

Yale shrugged it off and grabbed some Milky Ways from the kitchen.

"So what are you going to do with the money? How much did you get?" she finally asked.

She held the bite of Milky Way on the end of her tongue like a prayer.

"I don't really wanna say, I know that's weird. I just don't want to be treated differently. But it'll be enough to do all the renovations to this house I've wanted to do."

"That's great. Really great. You need to be careful though. I've read that winning the lottery can actually ruin lives."

What she said sounded as if it were coming out of someone else's mouth, like she had taken someone's argument but had left something out or twisted the message slightly. And her fervency made it sound that much emptier.

Then he looked very small, not his usual thickness. The sad kind of small.

"You know, when something like this really happens, something this monumental, it all seems very *normal.* Like turning on a light switch. It just gets absorbed into the mundane. I've already spent all the money in my head."

Macie wasn't sure what to say. She wasn't prepared to console her newly rich friend. "Remember when we used to go to the mall and plan who we were going to be while we were there? We'd pick out new names, accents, ages. When did we stop talking with accents?"

"Well, I stopped in middle school, but you haven't stopped yet," he said. "That's why I don't shop with you anymore."

*

Back in the car after finding some wine in the top cabinet of Yale's kitchen and actually celebrating with him, Macie wondered if she had peaked in college. She had nicer hair then. She had moved away from this town for a time.

Since when was she the type of person who believed in peaking too early? She blinked and focused on the road.

*

Yale's fortune had inspired her to clean her house. It was a small but necessary sort of inspiration. Bleaching the bathroom, dizzy with chemicals, the blank whiteness of it all smelled to her just like the indoor pool. She felt the clingy, clammy one-piece of childhood, the humid embarrassment.

The lottery winnings had also been a catalyst for adding a female to her small roster of friends. She figured her male-only companions proved an underlying mental condition. Macie had approached an unassuming figure in the library, the only other person who wanted to be in the library in the middle of a summer rainstorm that particular day.

The figure, Teryn, was laid back enough. Macie liked the way she used her middle finger to follow the lines on the book pages in the library. Teryn seemed willing to talk about books and paint fingernails. Those were Teryn's only advantages, really. Macie had tried to discuss books with Sven before, noticing a copy of *Tales of Burning Love* on his desk last winter. She got excited.

"Are you reading this book?" she asked Sven.

He shrugged. "This book, any book."

That was her last attempt.

A disadvantage of Teryn: Macie having to search for her emergency deodorant at the bottom of her purse near the unidentifiable crumbs while rushing to meet her at a restaurant. With the boys it didn't matter if she smelled from her bouts of nervous sweats.

Plus, Teryn's makeup was so thickly applied that it had to set up like a key lime pie. Teryn asked once to apply some blush to Macie's face, said she looked pale, and Macie shook her head in horror.

*

Macie stopped by the blue house on Blue Avenue occasionally to view the progress. New stained glass intended to look original, an addition with a study, Yale's recent habit of collecting snifters and beer steins. He had asked Raine to move out since he could afford the place by himself now.

Macie found a stack of opened envelopes on the dining room table after Raine had moved out.

"He left those for you," Yale said.

She found what she supposed was last year's Christmas cards that never reached her. One was from her great aunt in Youngstown. It was ornately glittered and had a rather smug looking angel floating on the front, crookedly smiling with eyes half shut.

Walking Backwards

She stares out the window at work for a good ten minutes and then down at her stringy hair. She would have to brush it eight times a day for it to be anything else, so she gave up before she began. Sort of like the Brownies in third grade.

*

I had thick, itchy tights. They were cable knit, but I didn't know it. I did know they were white. And so itchy. Leaves poked in them and got stuck as I rolled on the ground at recess. I got up and stared at the girls near me with brown sashes and matching skirts and even little fabric headbands. The headbands were all different colorful patterns that my mother would never buy me. "They would never stay in your hair. It's too slippery," she would say. I wanted to try still, but she refused. When I got back to class, the teacher pulled a leaf out of my hair. My stringy, slippery hair.

    I chewed on the end of my pencil until dismissal, slurping up the tangy, metallic spit about to escape from the corners of my mouth. I moved to the eraser, which just broke off into crumbly bits, impossible to remove from my tongue.

*

She races home to nothing. As she parks, she spots her neighbor out with his dog. He waves with one hand at her, the other hand clasping the cigar lodged in between his voluptuous, almost feminine lips. She thinks how she has never seen him without a cigar hanging from those pouty lips.

Her other neighbor is not outside but appears to be home. His truck is parked in the driveway, a Ford that states "FOR" very prominently on the back, the "D" a distant, faded friend. This neighbor is never home – always a charity, a benefit, a triathlon for cancer. It exhausts her to look at his shutters for too long.

She doesn't know either of the men beyond their apparent attributes. Thus, they are mere characters in a poorly written play, generalizable and categorizable. She likes this. She never talks, wants to keep it exactly this way.

*

The Brownies liked to French braid each other's hair and form secret clubs where they told anything but secrets. But they whispered and made codes on paper. I guess that made them secret.

I had you. I knew even then that Frank was an old man's name and you already seemed like one. You sat next to me in class. Our last names, Williams and Willis, meant that we were always together and always behind.

I hated you at first because you squinted in such a strange way, attempting to see the board all the way at the front. This annoyed me. Your face scrunched up like one of those dogs my cousin had with all the folds, wrinkles, whatever they were, all over the dog's body. I ignored you for a while until you drew me a picture of the teacher with boogers gushing out of her nose, filling up the classroom and drowning us all. I kept it in my desk, under my folder with the horses dancing all over it, so the teacher couldn't see.

*

Her brother calls as soon as she gets in the door, knows her schedule, probably has it under magnets on his refrigerator.

"Hey there."

"Hello."

"Having a good day?"

"Sure."

"Great. Well, Simone and I were thinking of coming up there next week. We've got some extra time off work and would love to go sightseeing around the city with you. You could be our little tour guide."

She somehow hears his grin. She knows he is amused

by the image of her in some khaki uniform, talking into a scratchy microphone, practiced in the art of walking backwards.

"I bet they have special muscles in their calves from doing that all day," she says.

"Huh?"

"Sure, that sounds great. Come down for the weekend. I can take off a few days." Her voice is bubbly, energetic, shrill; something coming out of her uncontrollably. Something she does not recognize.

"Yeah, I thought you might be able to. That's just great."

"What do you mean by that?" her voice snaps back.

"I-I don't know. I just thought you probably haven't taken your vacation yet. Sorry. I'll tell Simone the good news."

He hangs up.

She doesn't remember many societal rules, but she knows that you always say goodbye before you hang up, unless you are angry or filming a movie. And in the movie, there really isn't anyone on the other end.

*

You were over after school. We ran around the backyard. I couldn't catch up to you anymore so I walked into the kitchen, slamming the door, leaving you panting and staring at your shoes.

"We need a snack," I said to my mother.

"Okay, there are those teddy cookies you like in the pantry."

"Teddy Grahams," I corrected her.

I grabbed the box from the pantry. It was on a shelf I could actually reach along with those applesauce cups I took to school. Sometimes she forgot to give me a spoon and I had to stand in line with the kids who bought their lunch just to get one.

"Maybe that's what you'll serve at your wedding. Teddy Grahams."

"What?"

"You know, when you two get married someday. You and Frank. Grade school sweethearts," she sighed, "that's a story I always wanted for myself."

I marched outside, shoving Teddy Grahams into my mouth. I pulled apart the arms, legs, then the bear's head, discarding the rest of the carcass into the brown daggers of lawn. Mouth full of the others, I said to you, "My mom says you have to go home now."

*

"You won't believe who I saw the other day," her brother

says while cutting up his monstrous salad into manageable bites.

He sounds even more energetic in real life than over the phone. His wife is quiet and kind.

"Who?"

"Frank."

"*Frank*-Frank?" She looks up for the first time.

"Yeah. He was in the store ..."

She stops listening, thinking back to her mother and the ridiculous wedding bells ringing from her wide open mouth.

*

Frank was nothing but a sounding board, a mirror, a twin. After a fight in middle school about whether dogs were canines, she pretended to take a swing at his jaw, pinned him down on the carpet and kissed him straight on the lips. But it was a dry peck. She had been indoctrinated for so many years, to believe that she would want to. She did want to. But she kissed him like she would have kissed herself. Out of appreciation and playfulness and a bit of narcissism. No thundering feelings in her chest.

*

Her brother is still talking about something.

*

My grandma visited. She came inside with a puffy coat and many bags of gifts. She could have been mistaken for Santa but it was February and everyone knows Santa was underground somewhere waiting to see his shadow.

You were over and we were playing house in the living room, the place we really shouldn't have been because we would most likely break something. Grandma gave me some toys and I hugged her squishy roundness for a moment, running back to you in the living room. She shuffled into the kitchen to talk to my mom.

I ignored her and kept playing. She left, giving me a little wave from the front hall with her stubby fingers wiggling. I barely turned around to see her gesture and just kept on playing. Then suddenly I got the feeling there was a bag of marbles in my stomach and they were all spilling out. Some tried to climb up into my throat. A hurricane of marbles.

I don't remember much anymore. I do remember she smelled like potpourri and she had metal clips on her sleeves to keep them out of the way when she washed the dishes. I maybe saw her a handful of times after our day in the fragile living room.

*

He was still working on the salad.

"I forgot to look down at his finger though. Do you know if he's married? When's the last time you talked to him? You guys used to be inseparable."

He says this as if it's something new to her.

He turns to his wife and says, "I've never met people who were best friends like these."

She starts to think of the last time. An email, she thinks. She closes her eyes but all she can see is marbles shifting, reverberating, echoing in the expanse.

"What about you? When's the last time you talked to … your best friend? I bet, I bet you've been too busy eating clients and talking to sandwiches."

She gets up, walks across the room. Maybe to the bathroom, maybe to the parking lot to leave.

"I think you switched those around," he says to the tablecloth.

She drove to her home, still stuck on that grass made up of sharp blades, when the earth knew nothing of romance, and breathed deeply.

Coming of Age

When I drink heavily, I use words like "bildungsroman" in conversation, and that is the only time I find my dialogue worth hearing, though I may be the only one.

Previously Published

Thanks are given to the following publications in which these stories previously appeared:

Limestone Journal ('Bars of Soap'), *Bluestem Magazine* ('15 Signs of the Cocktail Generation'), *District Lit* ('Signs of Futility'), *Timber* ('Criminal'), *Hermeneutic Chaos* ('Craigslist Missed Connection'), *Maudlin House* ('RE: West Property'), *Cease, Cows* ('Compulsive Truths'), *Crab Fat Magazine* ('Cross-Pollination'), *Noctua Review* ('Of Course'), *Souvenir Lit Journal* ('Too Much of the Wrong Thing'), *Quarter After Eight* ('That'), *Knee-Jerk Magazine* ('Pirates'), *Clamor* ('Erase'), *Third Point Press* ('Talisman'), *Breakwater Review* ('Quilled'), *Liminoid Magazine* ('Projector'), *Referential Magazine* ('The Fire'), *Foliate Oak Literary Magazine* ('Back Row'), *Hackwriters* ('How to Become Unemployed (in 10 Easy Steps)'), *Monkeybicycle* ('Coming of Age').

About the Author

Claire Hopple lives in Asheville, North Carolina with her husband John. Her stories have appeared in *Hobart*, *Monkeybicycle*, *Bluestem*, *Quarter After Eight*, *Timber*, *Breakwater Review*, *Foliate Oak* and others. *Too Much of the Wrong Thing* is her first short story collection. Find more at clairehopple.com.

Acknowledgments

Thanks to my extremely patient and forgiving family, especially my parents (known as Ann and Scott to others), Erin, Travis, Maddy, Lucy, Houston, Harriet, Holly, Jack, Lynn, Jim, Audrey, Tom, Philip, Arline, Jane, Gregor, Ruby, Michael, Jackie, Erica, Curt, the Carpenters, the Duncans, and of course Unk and Nanna.

To the most influential writers: Lorrie Moore, Jonathan Lethem, Kurt Vonnegut, Joyce Carol Oates, Nathan Englander, Deborah Eisenberg, Sherman Alexie, John Edgar Wideman, Joan Didion, Amelia Gray, Christopher Merkner, ZZ Packer, Zach VandeZande, Laura van den Berg, Lauren Groff, and countless others.

To Matt Potter at Truth Serum Press and early editor Susan Hudson, who made all of this a whole lot more legitimate.

To my John Harlan, first reader and meal supplier, this book is basically yours.

Also from Truth Serum Press

http://truthserumpress.net/catalogue/

- *Track Tales* by Mercedes Webb-Pullman
  978-1-925536-35-5 (paperback) / 978-1-925536-36-2 (eBook)
- *True Truth Serum Vol. #1*
  978-1-925536-29-4 (paperback) / 978-1-925536-30-0 (eBook)
- *Wiser Truth Serum Vol. #2*

- *Deer Michigan* by Jack C. Buck
  978-1-925536-25-6 (paperback) / 978-1-925536-26-3 (eBook)
- *Hello Berlin!* by Jason S. Andrews
  978-1-925536-11-9 (paperback) / 978-1-925536-12-6 (eBook)
- *Luck and Other Truths* by Richard Mark Glover
  978-1-925101-77-5 (paperback) / 978-1-925536-04-1 (eBook)

Also from Truth Serum Press

http://truthserumpress.net/catalogue/

- *happymeat.us* by Kim Conklin
  978-1-925536-07-2 (paperback) / 978-1-925536-08-9 (eBook)
- *Rain Check* by Levi Andrew Noe
  978-1-925536-09-6 (paperback) / 978-1-925536-10-2 (eBook)
- *What Came Before* by Gay Degani
  978-1-925536-05-8 (paperback) / 978-1-925536-06-5 (eBook)

- *The Miracle of Small Things* by Guilie Castillo Oriard
  978-1-925101-73-7 (paperback) / 978-1-925101-74-4 (eBook)
- *La Ronde* by Townsend Walker
  978-1-925101-64-5 (paperback) / 978-1-925101-65-2 (eBook)
- *Based on True Stories* by Matt Potter
  978-1-925101-75-1 (paperback) / 978-1-925101-76-8 (eBook)

www.ingramcontent.com/pod-product-compliance
Lightning Source LLC
Chambersburg PA
CBHW031913190626
46814CB00003BA/1262